The Firehouse

THE FIREHOUSE

B. A. Trice

THE FIREHOUSE

iUniverse books may be ordered through booksellers or by contacting:

iUniverse LLC
1663 Liberty Drive
Bloomington, IN 47403
www.iuniverse.com
1-800-Authors (1-800-288-4677)

ISBN: 978-1-4917-3867-2 (sc)
ISBN: 978-1-4917-3868-9 (e)

Library of Congress Control Number: 2014911399

Printed in the United States of America.

iUniverse rev. date: 07/18/2014

1

One of the most intriguing things about the Firehouse was the floor. The entire floor was done in loose bricks—except for the very back, which was a smooth piece of poured concrete, like the floor of a garage or unfinished basement. These were old bricks, not the mass-produced and uniformly colored ones you might find today. These were different shades of red with brown and orange and even dark iron-blue—real old-time bricks. You could feel them move under your feet. You could hear them—and hear yourself walk on them. Your footfalls made noise; there was a click and scrape with every step. It was almost as if the place was alive. It drew you in, inviting you to take another step and then another, and you weren't just being drawn into the restaurant—there was a feeling of becoming part of it.

The back wall was brick, from floor to ceiling, with a service door that probably once opened to a back alley. Now it opened to a narrow, dark passage that led back to Lexington Avenue in one direction and up to Park Avenue in the other. Both ends were closed by a locked iron gate. One long wall was brick up to about shoulder height, where dark wood with brass accents took over, reaching to the ceiling, but the lighter colored bricks kept the place from being too dark.

The front was mostly doors. There were the two doors that had been used for the fire equipment, flanked by two walk-in doors. One now served as an emergency exit, and the other, now glass from top to bottom, served as the main entrance. The two main doors were the original wood, painted a dark red with white trim. They folded in upon themselves when opened. There was nothing fancy about them—they were thick and heavy but moved easily on their hardware and railings. The doors themselves weren't arched but had arched windows above them.

The building was as wide as three storefronts and had been there for well over a hundred years. It had seen the construction of Grand Central Station, the Chrysler Building, and the MetLife Building, which used to be the Pan Am Building back in the day. At one time, it was probably the northernmost firehouse in Manhattan, something that would have shocked the early fathers of the city who, folklore tells, decided not to adorn the north side of City Hall because they believed that Manhattan would never grow past Chambers Street.

The fourth wall was now mostly stainless steel and stove and a couple of tall coolers filled with drinks, all just behind the front counter. The grills were two big, mismatched Vulcan stoves that had probably seen action in a number of restaurants or diners around the city. Margaret had purchased both of them—used—at a good price. Above the grills were two large—no, *huge*—range hoods that vented the smoke into that back passageway and out of the building. They did an admirable job of keeping the air in the Firehouse clear, especially the upper floors.

Rich always wondered if the concrete section of floor in the back was where they once kept the horses that had been used to pull the fire wagons. Maybe there never were bricks there, or maybe the concrete replaced bricks that were removed in an earlier renovation, so that the area that might have been the stalls could be cleaned.

In any case, one thing always triggered a reaction, even from the regular customers—people that were in there every day—but especially from someone coming into the place for the first time. After taking a few steps inside, they would always look down.

It was the brick floor that set the place apart.

The one unfortunate thing about the place was that in an earlier renovation, part of the ceiling had been cut away to open the second floor into a loft that was now part of the seating area. The now open section was where the fire pole had been. In its place was a wide, wrought-iron, spiral staircase.

That pole would have really set the place apart.

"Where you gonna put these this winter?" Steve asked as he and his boss, Rich, stacked the last of the tables from the sidewalk. Steve had graduated from high school a couple of years ago and drifted from one part-time job to another.

"This winter?" Rich gave Steve his best *what are you talking about* look. "It's the middle of August, I'm sweating down to my socks, and you're wondering about this winter?"

They had just finished stacking the last of the six tables and twenty-four chairs, as they did every afternoon at closing time. In the kitchen, two other employees—a young in-between-ideas guy and a service worker in her thirties—cleaned the grill and put things in order. Early on, Rich was always surprised that no one had walked off with at least one of the chairs. Now, he didn't give it a moment's thought.

"I guess we'll stack everything in the cellar like we did last winter," Rich said.

"There's no room down there for all this! There's so much crap down there already!" Steve answered.

It took awhile to actually become a reality, but Margaret, the co-owner and Rich's friend, had gotten the idea of opening the Firehouse when she first saw it. It was an old fire station, vacant for many years. After the fire department moved to a larger building a block east, the building had first been turned into a bistro and then a coffeehouse, undergoing renovation and redecoration each time.

"Don't mention that junk down there, man!" Rich whispered. It was too late, and he knew it.

They'd known each other off and on for a couple of years and now, more and more, it seemed that he and Margaret could communicate more by a look or the tone of voice than by words; Rich thought that maybe this was how old married couples got along with each other.

"Hey, you know, we should start thinking about cleaning all that this weekend," Margaret said from behind the counter. She had just come downstairs with Doreen, Steve's mother, who also worked with them. Steve was amazed that she'd heard; Rich probably wanted to kick him.

"Does that mean we're staying?" Steve asked. "Does that mean I have a job for life?"

"You make it sound like a prison sentence," Margaret answered, wiping her hands.

"You might have a job as long as you keep working," Doreen warned. "You too, Tommy! Now get that trash gathered up, and don't forget to put out that bag of soda cans. It's recycling day tomorrow morning."

"Oh, Ma! You know that those cans never get picked up. I'm pretty sure someone comes by here in the middle of the night and takes them and sells them somewhere."

"What's it matter to you who gets them? Might as well help someone out who needs a little extra change—they all go to the same place in the end. If someone is industrious enough to take them, fine. I know *you'd* never have initiative enough to do something like that!"

Rich admired Doreen for the way she spoke her mind. She quickly became a sort of mother figure to everyone in the place. She was good with names and remembered faces, so, soon after meeting them, she would be calling people by their first names, asking how they were and about their families or their jobs.

After Margaret had rented it for almost a year, she and Rich took out a long-term lease on the old firehouse. That was six months ago. They both saw it as a long-term investment, and if things worked out they might someday think about purchasing the building if it became available. They had done well, and yes, it was time to clean out the cellar. From the very start, Margaret had planned to keep all of the cartons that had been used to pack the tableware, fixtures, and kitchen appliances. In the beginning, she was afraid that if she went bust and had to send it all back, it would be easier if they had kept the boxes. When Rich came on board, he'd insisted that if they went belly up, then everyone could just come and pick up the stuff because he'd be back in Wyoming.

Rich and Steve cleaned the grill and dining room while Doreen and Margaret took the cash drawer up to the apartment and prepared the deposit. Doreen was a wiz at bookkeeping. She loved to do what she called "pencil and paper, in-and-out accounting." The billing and payments were done electronically, so all Margaret had to do was keep track of things.

After the day's receipts were counted and the deposit slip prepared, they would bring the money bag down, and Rich and Steve would walk it down to the corner, to the Chase Bank across Third Avenue, and make the deposit. Everything was finished by four in the afternoon, which allowed time for Doreen to get home before rush hour and gave another kitchen worker enough time to get to one of her other waitressing jobs.

"How did we do today?" Rich asked Margaret.

Rich had a pretty good idea of how many burgers he'd grilled and served; after a couple of weeks, keeping count became second nature.

"Let's see," she answered, looking in the cooler where they kept the meat. "A couple hundred burgers—easy—and about twice that many dogs … about average, I guess. We ran out of lettuce, and I'm going to need another case of tomatoes before Thursday."

Thursday had been their biggest day in the past several months. They were closed on Fridays during much of the summer.

Surprisingly, the neighborhood provided a number of open spaces that provided shady places for people to spend their lunch hours. Grand Central was only a few blocks from the Firehouse, so they did a lot of business as the office workers poured into the streets looking for a quick lunch. There were also plenty of seats inside on the ground floor and in the open loft upstairs. They had also put tables and chairs out front. When the weather was pleasant, they could open the big wooden doors, opening the whole front of the restaurant to the sidewalk. Most of the people, however, seemed happiest to take their burgers and find a place to sit outside, scattering around the neighborhood.

Before long, they were attracting a crowd of regulars. They started recognizing people and learning names. A few came around daily, and others stopped in two or three days a week. They developed a solid business base.

When they were working, Rich called Margaret "M." Few of the customers knew her real name. In fact, most of the people, even the regulars, thought her name was Emily. She had tried Maggie, Peggy, Peg, even Margie and Margo for a while. None of them seemed to fit. Rich started calling her M—she liked it, and it stuck.

"Have you thought anymore about serving soup?" Steve asked as he finished tying the top of the last trash bag. Steve was the kind of guy that was always asking questions—not in an annoying way —he was honestly curious about a lot of things. He seemed to pick up on an idea and roll it around in his head until another thought took its place.

"I don't know," Margaret answered, leaning on the counter. "Maybe chili, but I don't want to turn this into a soup house. Once we get started, it may not end."

"I'd go for chili but not that Cincinnati five-way stuff," Rich said.

M gave him a dirty look. "You wouldn't know good five-way chili if it spilled in your lap."

"Five-way? What are you guys talking about?" Steve asked.

"Five-way chili, for you who did not grow up fortunate enough to experience life along the Ohio River—"

"This sounds like a Mark Twain story," Steve cut in.

"That's Ohio, not Mississippi—and don't interrupt while I'm taking chili. It basically means chili over spaghetti with cheese on top," Margaret continued, seeing Steve's eyes glaze at what was promising to be a long ode to one of Cincinnati's contributions to the world. "It's a lot more than that, but add beans, and you've got four-way, add chopped onions, and it's five-way. But I can see that neither of you are interested in being enlightened, so we'll just drop it for now."

"If you ask me—" Doreen started.

"Of course we are," Margaret said jokingly.

"This place isn't big enough for soup. I mean, people come in and grab a burger. Some of them eat standing up. Most of them carry out."

"So?" Rich asked as he tossed Steve a trash bag and pointed to an empty can.

"So, soup is sit-down food. People will hang around longer, and you won't get the same crowd turnover."

"You know, she's right," Margaret admitted.

Rich laughed. "Crowd turnover? Doreen, you're the best.

2

No one really knew whether it was curiosity or convenience that brought so many firefighters to the Firehouse. In a way, it seemed natural, like they were returning home, even though the place hadn't been an actual firehouse for more than forty years.

It had the feel of an old-time pub. There was just something comfortable about the place.

From the very beginning, Margaret had been quick to welcome all of them—firefighters, police, and emergency services personnel. It wasn't uncommon for guys from the new firehouse down the street to come in once they had finished taking care of their equipment after returning from a call. There were many times when several of them would sit in their boots, the bibs of their overalls folded down, having burgers. Many times, they arrived just before closing time, and no one made any effort to chase them out so that the tables could be bussed and the floor swept. Margaret had decided long ago that all of the public service people were good for business, and besides, they might need the fire department someday.

There were two large televisions suspended from the ceiling, one above the cash register and the other in a back corner. Margaret liked to tune one of them to a morning news show while she was getting things ready for lunch. The rest of the day, one was tuned to an all-sports channel and the other to an all-news network. Sometimes it was funny to watch the guys as they stared at the sets. There was little conversation. They appeared to be transfixed, staring at one of the two TVs like they were lost in a haze, especially after returning from a fire.

It was still a surprise when, in the middle of the second week of August, a fire captain and two lieutenants walked in one afternoon, just as they closed. The fire captain, like almost everyone who came into the place, looked at the floor after he took a few steps into the restaurant.

After making the introductions, Lt. Jenkins from the fire station down the street hesitated, as if he wasn't sure which of them he should be addressing. Finally he turned to Margaret. "We'd like to talk with you if you have a few minutes."

"Uh oh, I knew it—that grill of yours on the roof violates regulations. It was only a matter of time before they tracked you down, Rich," Steve said.

"Shut up!" Rich said, throwing a bar towel at him.

Lt. Jenkins continued, "We want you to help cater our Labor Day picnic. Every year, nine of our stations takes its turn catering the picnic. This is our turn, along with two others here in Manhattan, three houses in Brooklyn, and three in the Bronx. It's not on Labor Day—we hold it on the following Sunday. We just call it that. This year it's on Sunday the ninth. We'd like you to grill the burgers and hot dogs. We'll transport them, but we'll need you to get the buns and other stuff. The houses in the Bronx are doing all the side dishes, and the houses in Brooklyn have to arrange the drinks. We pay for everything, but we don't want to do the cooking—and it's better to have you do it than to trust it to a bunch of guys who can barely boil soup."

Margaret didn't hesitate before she agreed. It would be great advertising, and she didn't mind throwing in her labor to help out her friends.

A few days later, Lt. Jenkins came by and gave her a list of what they thought they would need and the details of how it would be picked up and delivered.

"If we're going to do this, then we'd like to do it all the way," Rich told him. "We'd like to be there to help serve the food. That way, we can be sure that our good name isn't being slandered by people throwing stuff around."

"That'll be fine by us. We'll still transport it out to the park, but you can come along and serve it, or at least supervise the serving—that is, if you want to lose most of your Sunday."

They had a great time. The picnic was held in Pelham Bay Park, and they served more than a thousand burgers and hot dogs. Margaret, Tommy, and Doreen went to the park to watch over the serving while Steve and Rich kept the grill going full blast at the Firehouse. Firefighters worked through the middle of the day shuttling the sandwiches from Midtown Manhattan to the park. Actually, they were flown there on a police helicopter from the Thirty-Fourth Street Heliport; to deliver them by car would have taken an hour. Steve voiced his disappointment that he hadn't volunteered to go to the park instead of Tommy—he'd never flown in a helicopter. At the same time, he admitted to Rich that he knew he was better at the grill than Tommy.

It was by far their biggest day, and they were surprised they were able to handle the numbers. Of course, it was good to be working with so many of the firefighters they had come to know. It was also good to make so many new friends. The weather was warm and humid but not as hot as the first days in September in New York City could be or had been in recent years. It turned out to be a long and exhausting but rewarding day.

That next Tuesday morning was bright and warm. It started out a little overcast, but the haze appeared to have cleared. Margaret realized that she had forgotten to get the salt she knew she needed. Before she started to get things organized, she walked the three blocks to the little supermarket on Third Avenue and picked up two five-pound bags.

On her way back to the Firehouse, she heard the jet before she saw it. It flew past Thirty-Eighth Street just as she turned the corner. *He's pretty low*, she thought. Every once in a while, depending on the landing patterns, a plane flew over Midtown. After awhile, you didn't notice. She didn't give it another thought as she let herself inside, locking the door behind her. It would remain locked until Doreen and Steve arrived at nine thirty.

There wasn't a great deal of work to do. Most things were done the afternoon before. Tommy had stocked coolers with cans of soda and beer and bottles of water. All of the napkin holders and the condiment containers had been filled. The biggest chore was to slice the onions and tomatoes and pull the heads of lettuce apart—and Pam would start on that as soon as she arrived at ten o'clock. All of the slicing was done by hand. Someday, maybe they would look into an electric slicer, if there was such a thing.

As usual, she had the television above her head turned to a morning news and talk show but only half listened to the various interviews, weather reports, and news reports.

She wasn't sure why she heard it. She was busy and usually didn't pay much attention to what was being said on the television, but there was urgency in the voice of the newscaster … something about a plane hitting the World Trade Center.

Margaret moved around to the front of the bar so she could see the screen, not knowing what to make of the report. As she watched along with millions of others around the world, the second airliner came into view, first flying past and then turning in order to strike the South Tower. She was stunned. Her knees went weak, and she almost collapsed. She had to hold onto the counter to keep herself on her feet. She couldn't take her eyes off the TV screen—she needed a cold drink.

At about that same time, she heard the sirens of the engine company down the street, figuring that they were responding to a fire somewhere—not imagining that they were one of the first responding companies.

"Are they headed down there?" she asked out loud. She didn't want to take her eyes away from the screen, but she went to the window. The ladder truck didn't drive past, and from the sound of the siren, they didn't go up Third Avenue but turned right and went down Second.

Steve arrived just before nine thirty, breathless, having run from the subway. He'd heard bits and pieces of the story and was anxious to get in front of a television. The story continued to unfold as camera crews began to arrive. Doreen arrived a few minutes later. The three of them just sat, as unbelieving as everyone else.

Rich arrived from the brokerage firm—where he worked what he called his "real job"—a few minutes earlier than usual. The office had closed, and everyone was sent home. The European markets had already closed, so there was no need for him to stick around any longer. The paperwork could wait—with everything that was happening, analyzing trade in the European stock market would be the last thing he'd want to think about.

After hearing the news, he'd stopped at the blood center in the Citicorp Building, figuring that one thing he could do to help was donate blood. It was on the way, and after all, he was type O negative, so he figured they might want him. But there was such a crowd already gathered in the waiting room that he just turned around and headed back to the Firehouse.

Midtown was full of people. Many, if not all, of the tall office buildings had closed, and the employees had spilled into the streets. Some were lucky and had gotten to the subways before they were shut down. None of the trains out of Grand Central were running by that time, and there were rumors that the tunnels and bridges were also closed, or would be closing

"I don't know whether we'll be busy or not. There are a lot of people out there with nowhere to go," Rich noted as he came through the door, already having pulled off his tie and jacket.

"Let's open and see what happens," Margaret answered, the most words she'd spoken in an hour. "Doreen, do you and Steve want to stay or go? You may have a tough time getting home later."

"I don't know what Steve wants to do, but no, I'll stay and take my chances," Doreen answered. "This place is probably as safe as any, and if you get busy, you'll need the help, especially if people have no place else to go." Steve said the same. Pam and Tommy arrived a few minutes later.

"I'm supposed to work a banquet at the Hyatt this evening, so I've got no other place to go until then either," Pam replied, answering the same question that Margaret had asked Doreen and Steve. Tommy just shrugged his shoulders.

Customers started to trickle in around eleven. The regulars knew there were televisions inside; they could sit and watch things happen while they waited and tried to figure out what to do next. By then, both Towers had collapsed.

Many sat all afternoon, in shock over what had happened. For many of them, there was nothing else to do. No one wanted to be out on the street. The offices in Midtown were all closed, and the trains out of Grand Central were not yet running. The magnitude of the disaster was beginning to sink in.

Some had lunch, lingering over their hamburgers and sodas. Most just sat and watched, along with Margaret, Steve, and Pam while Rich, Doreen, and Tommy took care of business.

Usually Doreen was bubbly while she worked, making chitchat with the customers, commenting on a new hairstyle or cut. Somehow she never missed noticing a new engagement ring and would tell the wearer how lucky the guy was to have her, or saying something like, "It was about time he asked you—and good for you to say yes!"

Today was different. She was somber. She still made the chitchat when she thought it appropriate, but a number of times Rich heard her praying under her breath, "God have mercy on those people … God have mercy." It wasn't long before he and Tommy joined in her prayers as they worked.

By early evening, a pall hung over the city. There were various reports coming in from the Pentagon and rural Pennsylvania, and the film footage was being shown again and again. *Air Force One*, carrying the president and the First Lady, had left Florida in the morning, and for a while, no one seemed to know where it had gone. Finally, reports that it had landed at the Strategic Command Headquarters, just outside of Omaha, came in. All other commercial aircraft had been diverted and then grounded. The skies were empty except for the military.

By six o'clock, long after their usual closing time, the last of the customers drifted out. Rich decided to take a bag of hamburgers down the street to the station. The guys that were there weren't in much better shape than the people they'd seen in the afternoon. Two of their brothers had been reported missing in the collapse of the South Tower. Seven were still down there, waiting for some news. The three who remained at the station sat in silence, watching the television and hoping for a miracle. They didn't feel like eating but thanked Rich for the sandwiches.

After they closed, Margaret and Rich walked to Grand Central with Doreen and Steve. Tommy lived downtown and walked home. Pam had called the Hyatt and was told that the banquet, a postelection celebration, had been canceled, so she made her way to the bus station and the ride back to Hoboken. Some of the subways were running, and Doreen could at least get to Steve's apartment. Margaret offered her the spare room in the apartment upstairs, but she declined, maybe a little more shaken than everyone else. She had two firefighters living on her block.

Midtown Manhattan was like a ghost town. There was no traffic on Lexington Avenue or Forty-Second Street. Grand Central was surrounded with members of the National Guard, and there were guardsmen in all of the intersections directing what little traffic there was as air guard, air force, or possibly even navy jets—it mattered little whose they were—crisscrossed over the city, patrolling. The roar of their engines provided an eerie but welcome and almost comforting assurance.

"Is there anything we can do?" Margaret asked one of the young guardsmen.

"No, just please go home," came the reply.

Later that evening, Margaret and Rich filled their backpacks with bottles of water and strolled around the neighborhood, handing out the bottles to guardsmen and police cadets who had been called upon to keep watch. Afterward, on the way home they stopped at the fire station. There were now more than a dozen firefighters there, the third shift having arrived and the guys from the early shift remaining.

"If anyone wants to stop by, we'll be happy to fire up the grill," Rich told them.

"I think we'll be okay," one of them answered, his voice hoarse. Margaret walked up to him and gave him a hug. There were hugs all around, along with a lot of tears.

"Anything we can do, let us know," she said.

"Thanks—that means a lot."

It was not until much later that evening that Margaret realized that the airliner she had seen that morning was the first plane, the one that hit the North Tower. It would be several more days before she and Rich realized how many of the new friends that they had made just two days earlier, along with the two old friends from the station down the street, had lost their lives that day.

In the evenings during the next few days, they continued their walks, handing out bottles of water to the guardsmen and police in the intersections and giving words of support and comfort and hugs to the emergency services personnel who had lost so many members of their family.

On Thursday evening, it began to rain and continued through the night, clearing much of the lingering dust and smoke out of the air. By Saturday, many if not most of the volunteer units that had arrived from across the country began to disperse. A new sort of sadness seemed to press upon those who continued to exhaust themselves with what was now seen as a recovery and no longer a rescue operation.

3

A lot of people thought Rich and Margaret were brother and sister—twins. They looked that much alike, although he was about an inch taller, just shy of six foot four. She was tall even for a girl from basketball-crazy Kentucky.

Both of them had dark hair, which they kept cut short, and both had the good looks of models—not high-fashion, runway-strutting supermodels, but all-American, kid-next-door good looks.

Neither of them liked to talk about their lives. They both were embarrassed by the fact that their pasts were so different, and their experience in New York was too much a cliché. "Too movie of the week," Margaret would say.

She had spent her years playing high school basketball, wearing a gray T-shirt under her uniform tank top, like Patrick Ewing during his time at Georgetown. The T-shirt played a practical role. Of course, she wanted to take the attention off her chest, but besides that, she perspired heavily—yet another thing she and Rich had in common. He told people he could sweat in the shower. They had spent many evenings after work just trying to dry off. Her mother used to tell her that it was just another of the things she'd inherited from her father, along with her height, her dark hair, and her love for sports.

Margaret was from Kenton Hills, Kentucky, just across the Ohio River from Cincinnati. She could turn on the southern charm and the accent at the drop of a hat, and a "y'all" slipped out every once in a while. A hundred and fifty years ago, she would have been considered a belle, living the easy life of a plantation owner's daughter. In truth, that was exactly the sort of life her mother and both grandmothers would have hoped she had … with debutante balls and young gentlemen callers. Margaret had seen her two older sisters go through that and was happy to act like the son her father never had. She chose sports over cotillions.

She didn't begrudge her mother for wanting her daughters to have a "belle of the ball" sort of life. The problem was that, to her, those lives often seemed so sad and tragic. Her sisters were happy, with successful, "well-bred" husbands. To Margaret, the line between blue blood and white trash was too often blurred, and she had no intention of making a bad choice and getting stuck on the wrong side of that line.

Being from Kentucky, Margaret grew up playing and loving basketball, just like her father, now a judge on the United States District Court of the Eastern District of Kentucky. A scholarship got her to the East Coast and the University of Rhode Island, which was overshadowed by the success of women's teams at neighboring Connecticut.

After riding the bench for part of her freshman year at URI, she played for three more years and graduated. School was always difficult. She was an average student—no more. Margaret graduated with a degree in business and corporate health. She wasn't sure what she would do with it, besides manage a health club somewhere.

There were plenty of opportunities available, and she took a long look at what part of the country she wanted to try next. Having never really experienced the West Coast, the idea of California had little appeal. Besides, she liked the idea of a change of seasons. It would have to be the Midwest or the Northeast. Living in Rhode Island had given her a feel for New England and the East Coast, so she decided it would be Boston, New York, Philadelphia, or maybe Baltimore but nothing south of that.

After several interviews, she took a job with the Nassau County Tennis Club on Long Island. She had the feeling that it would provide the best opportunity for advancement, and if she didn't like it, she'd have the experience and then move on. After two years, she grew tired of putting up with rich kids and their snobby parents treating her like a servant rather than the knowledgeable professional that she was. She started looking for something else, suddenly soured on the idea of managing a health club, or at least tired of managing a club in New York.

Margaret had played all those years with no serious injury, nothing that required surgery, so she had no scars, and since she had grown up before the era of a tattoo as a fashion accessory, she had none of those either. Her former roommate and best friend, Roxanne, talked her into having some model shots taken. She'd done it on a lark and received a phone call within a week.

Like so many models, she imagined that she couldn't survive on what she might make with a job here and a job there. But she was surprised to learn that she could make decent money—enough for a nice apartment while putting some away—and she found that she enjoyed bits of what New York had to offer.

To fill-in between modeling jobs, she had taken a job at the Oyster Bar in Grand Central Station. She had gone from serving drinks to managing the bar, but she kept looking for something different.

She did not have the desire to be a runway model and was realistic enough to know that the chances were slim. After all, she was simply too tall. Besides that, she had no chest. "Flat as a basketball court," she'd say. According to Roxanne, as well as the people at the agency, she had a perfect figure, but her breasts were small, especially in proportion to her height. She had several modeling jobs, good jobs—from the back, always from the back, and that was fine with her. She had been very self-conscious about her chest size in junior high and high school, and then, when she became more involved in basketball, it no longer seemed to matter.

You could see her in a magazine ad with a fur draped across her bare shoulders, or more often wearing a backless gown that neither she nor any of her friends back home could ever afford. She had appeared in several national fashion magazines and had built herself a respectable portfolio. Since she had no identifying marks, if you doubted it was her, she would have a tough time proving that it was. She would joke about some people being hand or foot models while she was a "back model." Too often when she referred to herself that way, people would misunderstand, thinking that she had said "black" and wonder about who she was referring to. Her most successful job was for a lingerie line. She was pictured from the back, standing in a bedroom, wearing only a pair of lace panties. The caption read, "Monica, is that you?" It was very successful, especially in Europe where those sorts of things were everyday sights.

"If you think about it, it was kind of silly," Rich would say. After all, who did this guy expect to find in his bedroom? Margaret never knew that Rich had torn a copy of the picture out of a magazine and kept it in his wallet.

Margaret was curious about his background. In the back of her mind, she thought he may have been gay. He lived alone, didn't date, and kept to himself … nothing wrong with any of that, though. One day she asked him quietly if he was an ex-con or someone on the run—witness protection maybe. She just wanted to know. He only laughed. It took about four visits to get him to talk and three more before she heard the whole story about Sandy. He and Margaret became best friends, and about that time, he started calling her M. On evenings that she didn't work, they would get together and take a walk. Sometimes they threw a few cans of beer and a couple of bottles of flavored seltzer in a little cooler with some paper cups and headed to the great room at Grand Central Station. There they would stake out an out-of-the-way corner and sit and listen to the musicians playing. Both of them would joke that the other was a cheap date.

4

One spring evening, during one of his runs through Central Park, Rich discovered the flowering magnolia trees and wisteria in full bloom. The area behind the Art Museum was full of trees and shrubs in bloom. By then, it was dark enough that he couldn't actually make out where the flowers were, but he found the air filled with a perfume that he hadn't experienced since the first time he'd driven through the orange groves south of Tucson.

He could hardly wait to walk through that area on the park's inner drive with Margaret. She was surprised that he was so excited about sharing the scent of flowers, but, as she got to know him better, Rich surprised her about a lot of things.

Like most people who had never actually been there until moving to the city, Rich's only knowledge and perception of New York came from television and movies. He was fascinated by the various neighborhoods that made up the city and was amazed by Central Park and the crowds that came there as an escape from their apartments and brownstones.

During one of his runs on a warm, sunny midweek afternoon, Rich couldn't believe how many people were out on the Great Lawn, taking in the sun. Even harder to believe were the huge crowds that filled the park on those evenings when there was a Shakespeare performance. He quickly learned to avoid the park on those days and instead ran along the bike path between the West Side Highway and the Hudson River. That route took him down along the southern tip of Manhattan, past the World Trade Center, through Battery Park, and back up along the East River toward the United Nations.

Rich told people that he was from fifty miles from nowhere, Wyoming. It wasn't too far from the truth. There was a lot of open space between Laramie and Cheyenne. Growing up, it wasn't uncommon to run across shepherds tending flocks of sheep on the still-open range.

Conner and Rachel Reiley owned a ranch where they raised cattle and three children, Richard, Robert, and Rebecca. "They're R kids," his dad would say, enjoying the play on words. Rich was proud of being a cowboy and used to tell people that he could probably outshoot and outride everyone in New York.

"Well, outride, anyway," he'd always add.

He grew up on an honest-to-goodness ranch. A ranch with a bunkhouse and hired hands and a spring roundup … right out of a western movie.

Until he was old enough to drive, the school bus would pick him up, along with his brother and sister, every morning at five after seven. Since they lived the longest distance from town, they were the first on the route—first on and last off. All through elementary and junior high school, he used the twice-daily, sixty-minute ride to read. Rich always had a book with him. The school librarian once joked that he was trying to wear out every book in the place.

A football scholarship got him to Arizona State. He could have gone to the University of Wyoming, but his parents talked him into going out of state.

"You can always come back, but if you never leave, you'll never know what's out there," his dad advised him. The older Reiley had been in the marines and served in Vietnam before returning to take over the ranch from his father.

Rich loved to play ball, and it had been his ticket to college. He also loved the ranch and the openness of the land in Wyoming, but he knew that he would someday have to find something else to do. He was also smart enough to know that he would never make football a career, so he studied hard and graduated in seven semesters with a degree in education, majoring in mathematics along with an endorsement in coaching.

Rich met Sandy during an after-game bar excursion. She was in her second year at Pima Community College, studying bookkeeping, and was out to celebrate some such thing with a group of her girlfriends.

Rich and a bunch of teammates had claimed a nearby table, and as the two groups began to meld, he found himself sitting next to this girl that didn't seem to be more that sixteen, petite and deeply tanned with long, black hair. They began talking, and as the night wore on and the crowded bar became more crowded, they found themselves sitting so close that they were practically sharing the same chair.

When everyone started to leave, Sandy asked him for his phone number and told him that she'd like to get together. He thought it was rather forward but wrote out his name and number on a napkin and handed it to her.

Rich had not dated much in high school; coming from a remote, small-town school, the opportunities had been few. There were girls around, but in a small school, everyone was just a good friend, and there was no real need for a date, formal or informal; groups of kids just got together.

He was surprised when Sandy phoned him the next week. They talked for almost an hour and ended by making a date for the following week, because he had an away game on Saturday.

They saw each other often, Sandy making a point to "drop by" campus at least once a week. She lived with her parents, and Rich began to enjoy going to her home on Sunday evenings for dinner and a chance to sit and watch a football game with her dad, away from "the animals" in the dorm.

At the end of football season in his senior year, Rich took his final semester exams. He had already been hired as a long-term substitute teacher and planned to move out of the players' dorm after the bowl game, during Christmas break.

There were a couple of guys from the team who were looking for a third roommate to share the rent of a little, three-bedroom house about six blocks north of campus. It was a block off Campbell Avenue and an easy bus ride to the middle school where he'd been hired. He could leave his truck parked in the driveway or on the street and not worry about finding parking on campus.

The house turned out to be a better deal than he'd expected. The front lawn, as in most older homes in Tucson, was brown grass and mostly white gravel, but there was a patio in the back with an eight-foot stone wall around it. A couple of orange and grapefruit trees and a fig tree provided the only green, besides the obligatory ornamental cacti and ocotillo.

"A good place for sunbathing naked," one of the guys told him—an image that Rich did not want to picture in his mind. Every so often, however, he'd come home in the afternoon to find a coed lying topless on one of the lounge chairs on the patio.

It turned out that it was in fact a very popular place for girlfriends to gather, Sandy included. Rich was uneasy about the whole situation, not wanting to be involved in some sort of place where wild, loud parties were held with people coming and going at all hours; he found that preparing for class took more concentration than he had expected. Those fears were without foundation, with both roommates being rather serious students, trying to finish up their own coursework and prepare for graduation.

The three of them had discussed the need for some sort of signal to be left in plain view, but that seemed too *Carnal Knowledge*, and they decided that they would all just respect each other's privacy. And he was surprised that they understood the reference to such an old movie. There were, however, a number of nights when Rich would come home late and find a couple entwined on the sofa in front of the television.

"Get a room," he'd say as he retreated to his bedroom.

He was always careful not to offend anyone since he was the invited third partner in the house. Neither did he want to raise an eyebrow or appear to make a judgment since Sandy often spent the night with him.

During his sophomore year, an assistant coach at ASU suggested that he enroll in a martial arts course, kickboxing and kendo—stick fighting. "It couldn't hurt, and it would give your temper an outlet while helping hone your skills," his coach had told him. Rich knew he had a quick temper, but he thought he kept it under control. At the same time, he was always afraid that it would get away from him during a game. Playing rover and free safety, he was expected to play with some abandon but always within limits.

Rich liked stick fighting. It was fast, and it helped his reflexes, but he really took to kickboxing, steadily advancing in skill levels.

After a game earlier that year, he and a group of other players headed for a bar. He was still underage, but many of the owners turned a blind eye to football players. In fact, they were usually happy to have them. Athletes attracted others and helped make a good night. One of his teammates, a six-foot-six, three-hundred-pound mountain of a starting offensive lineman took him aside and gave him some brotherly advice.

"Be careful. There's always some cowboy or biker who wants to prove how tough he is by taking on a football player. You'll have to learn to swallow a lot of crap," he warned. "You may be able to take that guy and maybe one of his friends—heck, you *know* you can take him, but you never know who might pull a knife or go out to his car and come back with a gun. Just be careful and travel in numbers—you watch our backs, and we'll watch yours."

It was good advice, and the guy was right—there were a lot of people out there who wanted a piece of a football player to prove their manhood. And the football team never obliged them—in a bar anyway.

Whether they made it a point to travel in packs or it just happened that way was never really clear. Rich couldn't remember ever going out when there weren't five or six other players around. They didn't go to the bars that often, and you wouldn't expect trouble in the sorts of places they frequented, but you never knew. Sometimes the biggest loud mouths were found in restaurants and fast-food joints. Someone might have been ready to take on one Wildcat, but when words were exchanged or a threat made, all of the teammates stood together, and no one was stupid enough to take on a group of five or six football players, especially when there were three-hundred-pound linemen and crazy-tough linebackers and safeties among the group.

In the third game of the season, during his junior year, against UCLA, the Arizona State quarterback was knocked out of the game by a late hit to the head and suffered a mild concussion.

During the next series, the Bruins ran a play-action pass. The tight end came across the middle, and just as the ball touched his fingers, Rich hit him and jarred the ball loose. The hit was so hard that he broke the player's collarbone and bruised his kidney.

The game was being televised nationally, and even the play-by-play announcers said it was a clean hit. Those were the sorts of things that happened to receivers trying to cross the middle of the field, they reminded their listeners. Many watching in the stands and on television were probably thinking that Rich was seeking payback for his injured quarterback. Some of the Los Angeles papers even echoed the accusation.

He wasn't thinking payback. Anyone who knew Rich knew that.

In an after-game interview, one of the coaches was asked if Rich had been given instructions to hurt somebody.

The coach replied that it was not the way they coached their players, and if Rich had intended to hurt someone, there would have been more than a busted collarbone.

From that game on, Rick carried a little more of a reputation and the admiration of the Arizona State faithful, and suddenly he was considered one the toughest on the team. Besides all that, he led the Pac-Ten in interceptions during his junior year.

Two weeks after graduation, Rich married Sandy, whom he had dated regularly since the beginning of his junior year in Tucson. He had already secured a job in Page, Arizona, where she had also found a job. He would be teaching math in the middle school and coaching the high school football team. Rich was happy and hoped Sandy would be happy also.

They rented a three-bedroom house on the northern edge of what had been a modern and precisely laid-out town in 1956, when work on Glen Canyon Dam had started. Sandy had already been working in the accounting department of the power plant located a few miles east of town.

Rich could look out the living room window and see parts of Glen Canyon and Lake Powell. He loved the wide-open spaces and the seemingly endless sky.

Page was a resort town on the highest order. During the summer months, it was busy, and a large percentage of the people were involved in some way with the surrounding canyons, the dam, or recreation on Lake Powell. Rich spent his first summer there teaching drivers' education and learning to waterski.

During the winter months, things slowed down dramatically. Many of the businesses closed as winter settled in on the high plateaus of Northern Arizona and Utah.

For the first time in her life, Sandy was two hundred miles from a city. As it turned out, it might just as well have been a million miles.

After two years in Page, things started to go sour. Sandy was used to a faster pace in Tucson. Things were happening too slowly, especially as they prepared to spend their second long winter together. She wanted to go out for dinner, get together with friends, go shopping. None of that was readily available in Page, and she made little effort to make new friends, even though the towns' people were quick to welcome her husband and would have welcomed her. She even found it difficult to get to know the people at work.

They talked about it. He said that he didn't mind her driving down to Phoenix or Tucson for a weekend when she wanted. Rich was home every evening, arriving only a few minutes after she got home. He was happy to go with her when he could and spend a weekend visiting her parents or traveling to Las Vegas, Phoenix, or Salt Lake City for the weekend. He even told her he would start looking for a teaching job somewhere else if that would help. He tried everything, but it never seemed to be enough to satisfy her.

When Rich came home after football practice one night in early November, Sandy was gone. She'd packed her clothes and left—with no word. Rich had known that she wasn't happy but never suspected that she'd leave—not like that.

There were frantic calls to the police and hospitals, with no results. She'd been seen, alone, at a gas station earlier in the day when she should have been at work, but there were no other clues.

Rich spent the next week just trying to track her down. Calls to her parents and friends came up empty. He even hired a private investigator to try to find her—nothing. Finally, after three weeks, she phoned.

"I'm in California," she confessed.

She would not tell him where. She called to say that she was fine and safe and just trying to figure things out. She made the same phone call to her parents. Rich would find out much later that she did not say anything about the fact that she had already petitioned to change her name and was even in the process of changing her social security number.

The whole thing took its toll. Rich lost weight and could not keep his mind on coaching. Luckily there were only a couple of weeks left in the season, and the assistant coaches helped take up the slack. Page was small enough that everyone soon knew what had happened. The teachers and principal were supportive, but Rich just sort of closed in upon himself.

He spent most of the next summer trying to find her. None of her friends knew where she was, and none of them knew where she might be.

Rich went through the motions of teaching and coaching through the next year. It had been more than a year since he'd heard from Sandy. He had to make a change. In the spring, he let the administrators know that he would not be back in the fall. When the semester ended, he sold the furniture, packed his things, and moved back to Wyoming.

Once back on the ranch and around people he had known all his life, Rich began to feel just a little bit better. He was back on a horse and helped work cattle through the summer and the fall roundup and then slept most of the winter. He started to grow a beard, but it came in gray and grizzled looking, so he shaved it off, feeling even more empty.

He had tried to find help. He knew that he was suffering from some sort of depression, and it scared him. He needed to move on.

A friend from Arizona State helped him find a job as an entry-level stock analyst in Phoenix. His ability with numbers helped him fit into the job. After almost a year there, he found an opening with the company's home office in New York and thought a bigger change would do him good.

He made one last swing through Tucson to try to find Sandy, with no luck. He spoke with her parents, Bill and Lauren, promising that he would call often for news, and they promised to keep him informed.

He sold his truck, packed his things one more time, and headed east, hoping for that new start. He still wore his wedding ring, although he had a feeling in the pit of his stomach that his marriage was finished.

The job was perfect. He was asked to keep track of foreign investments and the European stock market. His knowledge of Spanish helped him, especially in dealing with customers in Spain and the Madrid branch. The hours were good also. As he became more involved with the European markets, he was expected to keep their hours, so he would arrive at work at three in the morning and leave by eleven, after the European markets had closed and he had compiled the data.

In the afternoons, he took walks, long walks—something he had never done before. He was beginning to feel life coming back into him. He called Sandy's parents weekly—still no word.

He enjoyed the job, and he was making good money, but he realized that his life was empty, just as empty as it had been back in Arizona. He decided that he needed to get out of the apartment in the evenings and meet some people, put himself back into circulation. He started to visit some of the various ethnic restaurants in different parts of the city. With his hours, he could catch a late lunch or an early dinner, both times when places weren't very busy. He found a couple of Chinese as well as Middle Eastern places that he really liked and began frequenting them.

One afternoon, he stumbled onto the Oyster Bar, the huge restaurant in the lower level of Grand Central Station. He was amazed at the place. He had never seen a raw bar before but was interested in trying new things. After that one try, Rich decided he would pass on the raw oysters but found the restaurant's lounge, with its vaulted ceilings, interesting.

That's where he and Margaret first met. After another couple of weeks, they found that they lived only a few blocks from each other, and since it was never crowded when he was there, he would sit at the bar lingering over a glass of beer, and they would chat. A lot of the people who saw them thought he was a guy coming to keep his sister company in the late afternoon before the evening rush.

They never actually dated, but one Friday evening Rich stopped at the Oyster Bar on his way from a movie and offered to walk her home. She accepted, and it became a usual thing. She wasn't seeing anyone, so it was fun having someone to talk to outside of work.

After Margaret had gotten to know him, she talked him into doing some photo shoots with her. She told him about the people with whom she worked and wanted to introduce him to them. "You can never have too many friends, and it'll be fun," she told him. Margaret knew that a lot of people at the restaurant thought they were twins; in fact, that's how she introduced him to some of her friends.

He actually got a couple of calls. He refused to do any headshots but did let her talk him into doing some body shots like she had done—from the back or with another head pasted digitally on his body. He was sinewy, not muscle bound—more Rowdy Yates than Rambo. He though it was silly, but he liked the extra money. The search for Sandy had been and continued to be expensive. Pictures of his torso could be seen around the country—from the back, with a television perched on his shoulder, and from the front, in a couple of ads for milk, from his nose down, showing off his milk mustache and physique, or sometimes with a well-known sports figure's head sitting on his shoulders, or knees to neck, dressed in a tux, adjusting a shirt cuff. He joked that he was happy to have two jobs where only one of them forced him to use his head.

5

For the first year, Margaret leased the building, wanting to see how things went before she thought about buying it outright. The first months were rough. It took a long time to get established, but then something caught on, and things got busy—very busy. She made it into the city's Restaurant Guide, but it wasn't until the *New York Times* ran an article on the Firehouse, in the Wednesday Food Section, that things sort of exploded. During the three weeks that followed, it was unbelievable, and they thought they wouldn't be able to keep up. Then it slowed, finding a balance. They were still very busy, but it was a steady busy that became more manageable.

She realized that she was doing well but working too hard. She'd hired a couple more people, but she was there every day, and it began to take its toll.

One afternoon, she called Rich. They hadn't seen each other very often since she left the Oyster Bar. Their paths had simply stopped crossing, but she remembered that he used to talk about missing burgers like the ones he could get at the cafes back home—"Big, greasy burgers and fries. How can a city as big as New York not have a place where you can order a big burger and a pile of french fries?"

She talked him into joining her. He wouldn't have to give up the job at the brokerage house if he could arrange to get out of there by eleven thirty. He said he'd give it a try and had never regretted the decision.

After almost three months of working together, she invited him to move in with her in the apartment above the Firehouse. She was renting the whole building. Their hours were so different that they would hardly see each other outside of flipping burgers in the afternoon, and she had extra rooms. There was no sense of her having all that space and for him to be paying rent somewhere else. It took Rich awhile, but finally he agreed, only after he told her that he had no intention of making it anything but an arrangement between roommates and that he did not see it as "moving in and living together." He would pay his share of the rent and carry his share of the load. Once he settled in, he liked the plan. His new bedroom was about as big as the studio apartment in which he had been living, robbing him of rent money every month. Eventually, he bought into the restaurant as well.

They never really talked about the living arrangements. The third-floor apartment ran the length and width of the building. It was an enormous room and had been home to a company of twelve firemen before the first set of renovations enclosed some of the open spaces.

There were now three bedrooms with a large bathroom in the back, the type you'd find in a small locker room. Even though it would have been a major undertaking, Margaret mentioned that she didn't understand why it hadn't been remodeled. The shower was separated from the rest of the room by a dividing wall. It was essentially a separate, twelve-by-eight-foot room. It was covered ceiling to floor with white ceramic tiles and had four shower heads. You had to step over an eight-inch threshold to get into it. One would suppose that with four guys in there showering at once, there would be a lot of water on the floor, but there never was or seemed to be. The floor of the shower was covered in the same bricks as the main floor. At first it was strange to walk on them. They were rough and uneven, but they provided the ultimate nonslip surface, and after a couple of times, except for that familiar and welcome feeling of movement under your feet, walking on them barefooted seemed natural.

Curiosity got the better of Rich. One day, on the way back from the office, he picked up a piece of artists' charcoal and some drawing paper. After they closed the restaurant, but before he showered, he made a rubbing of the floor so he could replicate the pattern. Then he pulled up about three square feet of the bricks. He found that they sat on a foundation of mortar or concrete that was deeply grooved with channels that funneled the water to the drain. Replacing the bricks, he realized a deeper appreciation for whoever had designed and built the place.

Someone along the way had changed one of the shower heads in the far back corner with one that hung out from the wall about three feet. It was eighteen inches across, nickel-plated, and looked expensive. Margaret loved it. The apartment had terrific water pressure in spite of the fact that it was on the third floor and plenty of hot water, owing to the huge boiler in the cellar. Standing under that shower was like standing under a waterfall. Rich had exchanged the one on the opposite wall with a fancy, adjustable showerhead, which Margaret also loved using. It had a dozen different settings from mist to jet, and with the water pressure, you had to be careful that it didn't try to peel your skin off.

Between the wall of the shower and the long wall of the bathroom was a small space with a window that now faced the side of the next building and was useless for light or ventilation. Above the window, however, was a powerful exhaust fan.

In the other half of the room were three toilet stalls, a couple of urinals, and four wash basins. On the other side of the long hallway, opposite the bathroom, the other half of the space was divided into a kitchen and two of the bedrooms.

The open room that remained acted as their living and dining areas. Margaret had furnished it with a large antique oak table and chairs, a couple of comfortable recliners, and a sofa. The big room faced the street; the bedrooms were toward the back.

There was a pair of metal doors with reinforced glass windows. They opened onto a terrace that hung halfway over the sidewalk, facing north and uptown. This is where, in the old days, hay for the horses had been hoisted into the loft that had been on the second floor. When the doors were opened, which they were much of the time, they let in plenty of air, and in the evening after the traffic had slowed, even the noise of the city seemed distant—which was surprising and seemed impossible when compared to the going and coming and traffic during the day.

Outside the doors, the terrace was surrounded by a black, wrought-iron railing that gave the place a French Quarter look. Margaret found a folding oriental silk screen for privacy. Rich installed a pair of sliding screen doors to keep the bugs out, and for security, he bolted on another set of wrought-iron bars, enclosing the entire terrace.

One strange thing about the third floor was that it was full of skylights. There were five scattered throughout the apartment. All five were about six feet long and three feet wide and filled with frosted glass. All of them let in a surprising amount of light … enough in fact that the potted fern that Margaret had placed in a corner of the shower seemed to thrive.

Rich and Margaret both understood that they had been installed during one of the renovations. During part of the day, they let in a tremendous amount of light, which would have made it difficult for off-duty firefighters to sleep in what was probably, originally, a mostly open-spaced dormitory. Over the decades, as taller buildings were built, there was still plenty of light at certain times of the day, but during late fall, winter, and early spring, no light got through after about four in the afternoon. Still, whoever had done the installation had done a good job. They were placed where they now gave the most benefit, and there were no signs of them leaking.

On one of their trips to Montauk, Rich returned carrying what must have been at least a hundred pounds of rocks … each roughly the size of a softball.

"Good thing they don't have a weight limit on the Jitney!" Margaret told him.

They were beautiful stones—round and a little flattened, having been ground, tumbled, and polished by the waves and sand since creation. He scattered them along the walls of the shower. The various shades of gray, brown, and yellow took the harshness out of all the white tiles.

He was especially proud of finding what must have been, judging by its color and texture, a brick. It was about the size of his fist but had the shape of a baseball that had been flattened just out of round. Instead of going into the shower, it found a place in the cabinet on which the television now sat, along with a fish bowl being filled slowly, trip by trip, with pieces of sea glass that fascinated Rich beyond Margaret's belief.

Soon after moving in, Rich installed several overhead fans. They made an immense difference in cooling the rooms, helping the single, large-capacity, window air conditioner make the place bearable during the summer.

In the evening after they had washed off the day's grease and the smell of smoke from grilling and serving hamburgers and fries, and if he didn't go to the gym, Rich would usually spend part of the night sitting at the table and reading while Margaret staked out the sofa in front of his only real contribution to the furniture, a large-screen television. Sometimes, on really warm evenings, they sat on the roof where a little patio deck had been built during one of the earlier renovations. Even though tall buildings surrounded the Firehouse, there was usually a nice breeze in the evening and some pretty good sun for a couple of hours during the afternoons.

Rich never had been a big fan of television. The only things he regularly watched were the first minutes of *Monday Night Football*, until the starting time was changed to nine o'clock, and college games on Saturdays and the pros on Sunday, or baseball when his beloved St. Louis Cardinals were playing—that is, when the weather kept him inside.

Two evenings a week, Rich taught or led a kickboxing class at the Grand Central Sports Club. It wasn't actually a martial arts class but more like aerobics for people looking for something different from the usual exercises. He didn't do it to be paid but for the chance to get both Margaret and him a free membership. On the other nights that he worked out, he jogged up to Central Park, ran halfway round the inner drive to Eighty-Fifth Street, and then ran wind sprints back to the club. Flat-out for a block and then walk a block all the way back to the club on Forty-Third Street.

He liked to life weights and take a steam, just to keep in shape; Pushing thirty, he was afraid of developing a paunch. Even though weight issues didn't run in his family, he had seen too many of his friends, ex-teammates, go from muscle to flab. Margaret liked to swim and use the stair machines. Often they would go to the club together, but she finished before he did, so she usually went home alone, giving him time to work out after his class.

On the weekend, when the weather was good, and neither of them were involved in a photo shoot, they headed for one of the beaches, oftentimes farther out on Long Island.

In his old apartment, Rich used the television for background noise while he was busy doing something else. Sometimes, however, he would sit and watch a program with Margaret. Every once in a while, they rented a movie and watched it together. One more thing that surprised Margaret about him was the fact that he was partial to the big epics, old classics, and film noir while Margaret liked anything. They both enjoyed watching what the other had chosen.

His hours at the firm forced him to go to bed early. He usually went to his room before eight and was asleep before eight thirty, sometimes earlier. He woke at two o'clock in the morning to get to the office before three when the European stock markets opened.

When they sat together, Rich would pick Margaret's legs up off the sofa and swing in underneath them, placing them across his lap, sort of like swinging a gate open and closed. Once, after she sprained her ankle, he spent the evening icing and rubbing it. The rubbing became a sort of ritual when they would sit together. With his huge and powerful hands, once or twice a week Rich would, almost absentmindedly, sit and give her feet what Margaret described to her friends as a "to-die-for massage."

After the doors were locked and the lights turned off, they climbed the two flights of stairs to the apartment—they never called it "their apartment," even after they had shared it for a couple of months.

It was true that after he'd moved in they hardly saw each other outside of work. He was out of the house by two thirty in the morning and back around eleven. He'd quickly change clothes and be ready at the grill just before noon. His office was in the fifties on Park Avenue, and unless it was raining hard, he walked both ways.

At first, Margaret would wake up when she heard him getting ready to leave in the morning, just to say hello. She liked the idea of being able to go back to bed after he left; it felt like she was getting away with something. He was going to work, and she was going back to bed. That didn't last more than a couple of days. After that, he tried to be a little quieter, but if he woke her, she didn't stir.

During the first couple of weeks, they were overprotective of each other's privacy. After awhile, things became more relaxed, and both of them became more comfortable with the way things were.

The layout of the bathroom offered enough privacy. You couldn't see into the shower unless you actually stood at the door and looked in. A number of times, they had both accidently flushed a toilet and caught the other in there.

There were also a number of times when he would be standing at one sink, shaving, while she used another mirror to put finishing touches on her makeup. After awhile, it had become natural. They had both grown up sharing a bathroom with siblings and had experienced the coming and going of a college dorm.

One Saturday morning, Margaret went to take a shower. She hadn't heard Rich and thought he was still asleep. Later, she realized that she must have been half asleep herself because she didn't notice his bathrobe hanging on the hook outside the shower.

He had the habit of standing under the shower for only a few moments, getting wet and then turning off the water while he soaped himself and washed. Some people called it a navy shower, a way to conserve water; his teammates at the university called it weird. Rich would explain that growing up on the ranch, it was often necessary to save water, and it was not so unusual to take a bucket, towel, and a bar of soap out to the water trough behind the barn, strip down, and wash there. It was just something that he was used to doing. Even at the university, he kept up the habit of turning off the shower, although there never seemed to be a shortage of water in the locker room or the dorm. With the water turned off, he often shaved in the shower as well—killing two birds, he'd say.

Margaret stepped out of her bathrobe and hung it and her towel on the hook, next to his, still not noticing that it was there, and stepped into the shower. There he was, covered with soap suds, braced against the wall with his left hand while he washed his left foot with his right hand. Luckily he had his back to her as she stood there, naked, staring at him.

It took a moment for her to come out of her daze, and she quickly stepped out and put on her robe, thankful that he hadn't seen or heard her—she thought. Not that she would have cared about being seen, but she was embarrassed about walking in on him.

Rich saw that she'd turned on the light—the skylight had offered enough light for him that morning. He'd heard her come in but paid no attention. It was not uncommon for both of them to come in and use the sink or toilet while the other was in the shower.

He wanted to say something clever but thought better of it. "I'll be finished in a minute," he said as she grabbed her towel.

He tapped on her door as he left the bathroom. "All yours."

"You know, most normal people find it easier to take a shower with the water running," she answered through the door.

"Sorry. I'll sing or whistle or something next time. It's big enough—I suppose there's room in there for both of us at once."

"Well, I must say, covered with soap suds, you still looked pretty hot. I didn't think you saw me." She laughed as she opened her door. "I might tell Neil to find you some soap ads."

"Oh no you won't! And I didn't see you. I heard you gasp. What? Was I doing it wrong? Did you see something that surprised you—like those 'Monica, is that you?' ads that you did?" he joked, joining her laughter.

On Monday evening after work, she found a high-tech shower radio with a clock and CD player. On a piece of paper, he'd written: *In order to avoid future embarrassing situations, and for listening to the news on Saturday mornings.*

6

When in for the evening, Rich's usual choice of dress was a pair of gym shorts, a T-shirt, and a pair of heavy flip-flops that he'd picked up during a game trip to Honolulu. When it was really cold, he would put on a pair of sweatpants and a sweatshirt. On really warm evenings, he went shirtless in the apartment.

Margaret, too, would spend the evening in a pair of shorts and a T-shirt or sweatpants and a sweatshirt.

On one of those very warm evenings, she walked into the room wearing only shorts. Rich didn't look up from his book. Margaret, feeling a little miffed, sat on the sofa in silence, reading a magazine—still with no reaction from Rich. After about fifteen minutes, Rich broke the silence, still not looking up from his book.

"Do you want me to put on a shirt?"

"What?" Margaret answered.

"You know that I grew up on a ranch, used to play football, lived in a dorm, shared a house with other players, and was married."

Looking over the top of her magazine she asked, "So?"

"Well, if you want a reaction from me, you won't get one."

"I was hoping for a catcall or a wolf whistle or something."

"I don't wolf whistle, and to be honest with you, right now it's all I can do to sit in my chair without falling off. You want a reaction from me? Take a look at my eyes trying to pop out of my head!"

He got up from the table, went to the refrigerator, and picked up a beer and a bottle of seltzer, taking one to Margaret, still sitting on the sofa, topless.

"Here, buddy," he said, handing her the seltzer as she reached for the bottle of beer in his other hand. "I think you're a lot better developed across the chest. I think your shoulders could use some work though. I'd be happy to help you with that."

Margaret laughed as she moved her feet so that he could sit down, taking a drink.

"You know, you can run around here buck naked for all I care. It's your apartment, after all. Do you want me to go first?" he asked as he hooked his thumb in his shorts, pulling them down, revealing the top of his left cheek. He lifted her legs across his lap as he sat down.

"You'd like that, wouldn't you?" She gave him a little kick.

"Just up here, or would you be topless downstairs too? That might help business, but I think we'd have to get a different sort of license."

Margaret kicked him again.

"Well, I have to admit I'd probably get a lot less work done," he continued with a leer, looking over his reading glasses.

Margaret gave him a look of disbelief. "Richard Reiley, that's the nicest thing that you've ever said to me!"

She thought Rich looked confused, not realizing what he'd said, at first. Then it must have dawned on him, and he quickly got up from the sofa and, rather sheepishly, retreated back to the table.

Margaret got up, went into her bedroom, and put on a T-shirt. As she headed back to the sofa, she slipped around the table and put her arms around Rich's neck. "Sorry," she said, giving him a kiss on the temple.

He put down the book and took her hands in his.

"Don't be. I shouldn't have said what I said. But, honest, if you want me to put on a shirt, I'll do it. If you want to run around here topless, do it. It's your house."

"It's our house, Rich, or at least I want it to be. And no, you don't have to put on a shirt unless you want to. I like looking at you.

Most girls would kill for a chance to see your six-pack and those veins and ligaments—whatever they are—on a regular basis, and I have it every night. I'm the luckiest gal in the city!" She ran her hand across his chest and patted his belly. "The only thing I think I like better is seeing you out and about in a white T-shirt and jeans, but here, there's nothing I like better than getting an eyeful just the way you are right now."

He didn't move. It seemed like forever, but it was only a few seconds. She gave him another kiss as he got up from the table and went into his room. She followed and then knocked on the open door and watched as he put on a T-shirt.

"It *is* your house, your home too," she said as she stepped in his room. "And please, you don't have to do that for me. I don't mind, really."

A tear ran down his cheek as he turned away from her. He quickly wiped it with the palm of his hand.

"Hey, what's wrong?" she asked.

"You know, I would love for us to take this to the next level—you know I would. But right now, even after all these years, I just can't. I can't let go of her. I know I should. I know I should find a lawyer and get a divorce or whatever has to happen to make it legal and put an end to it. I just can't. I know—I mean … I hope you understand."

"Of course I understand. Well, I *think* I do … but at the same time, I want to, but I can't. I mean—I guess I don't know what I mean."

She took a step toward him, put her arms around him, and gave him a hug, resting her chin on his shoulder. After a long moment, he returned the embrace and kissed her cheek before letting go. She sensed that he was uncomfortable, so she released her hold on him and turned to leave.

"I'm sorry," he whispered as he reached and touched her hand.

"I am too," Margaret answered, wiping a tear from her cheek.

Margaret realized right then that she hated Sandy—a woman she'd never met. She had been gone for almost four years, and she still controlled his life. She wanted to tell him to let Sandy go, to take off the ring, get a divorce, and get on with his life. She had wanted to tell him that since she first heard the story. She hated to watch him let his life slip by.

7

About three weeks after Rich moved in, Margaret received a phone call from an old teammate at URI. Margaret told Rich that Roxanne had been her roommate all four years at the university. She was now teaching art at a girls' prep school in Pawtucket. Her husband, Stan, a partner in an accounting firm in Providence, was coming to New York the following Thursday morning for a meeting with one of the firm's clients. Roxanne was planning to come to New York and join him on Saturday morning, and she hoped that they could all get together that evening for dinner.

Margaret asked Rich if he minded if she asked Stan to stay in the apartment, and then Roxanne could join him.

"Of course, but please don't feel that you have to ask," he replied. "It's your place, and they're your friends. I look forward to meeting them."

"I do have to ask. This is your home, too, and it wouldn't be fair if I just invited someone without talking to you first."

Margaret phoned and invited Stan to stay with them while he was in the city. Roxanne could catch up with him on Saturday. They'd do some shopping and then have dinner.

Stan arrived after his meetings were finished on Thursday. He'd called earlier and told Margaret that he was having dinner with clients and would be there around nine.

Rich waited up long enough to welcome him.

"Hey, Marvelous!" Stan said as he kissed Margaret hello.

"Marvelous?" Rich asked.

"You didn't know?" Stan shook Rich's hand. "That was her nickname at URI—because that's what she was on the court. You've been together for how long, and she didn't tell you? Richard, my man, the two of us are going to have a long talk."

Margaret interrupted, "Okay, enough. We can talk about that later."

Rich put his hand on her shoulder. "Well, I've always known she was marvelous. I'll take a rain check on that talk. Right now I have to get to bed. Good night."

"Did he do that for show?" Stan asked, noticing that Rich went into the third bedroom. Stan and Roxanne had stayed in the apartment before Rich moved in, so he knew which room was Margaret's.

"No, that's his room. He insisted on it when he moved in. I told you and Rox that we were sharing the apartment but we weren't living together. Didn't you believe me?"

"We—I didn't know what to believe. Actually, I'm surprised, but if that's the way it is, who am I to judge?" Margaret and Stan talked for another hour before she admitted that she was exhausted.

"I hope I don't have to tell you to make yourself at home. You know where everything is. Rich will be up and out before three. I usually don't hear him—you probably won't either."

"I'm gonna watch the news and then go to bed," replied Stan. "I have a seven-thirty meeting in the morning. Will I see you?"

"Oh, I'll be up by then and will have coffee made if you want it."

Rich and Stan didn't see anymore of each other until Friday evening when he returned from his meeting. They sat up until the early hours of the morning drinking beer and talking about nothing in particular.

The three of them walked to Grand Central Station to meet Roxanne when she arrived on the nine o'clock train, and then they went to a bagel place on Third Avenue for brunch.

Rich was surprised. No one had told him that Roxanne was African American. Why would they? It would never have occurred to Stan or Margaret to bring it up.

She was as tall as Rich, which added to the surprise. For a woman who was as tall and as "big" as she was, she was also stunningly beautiful, moving with the fluidity of a natural athlete. She didn't walk; she seemed to almost float or glide along, her long, black hair bouncing with each stride. She reminded him of someone from television, but he couldn't put his finger on who. Roxanne was heavier than Margaret by maybe twenty pounds, and Rich decided he would not want to find himself on her bad side.

Stan said that he wanted to return to the office for a couple of hours. Roxanne and Margaret wanted to start their shopping, and Rich was left free for the rest of the afternoon. He knew better than to offer to tag along with the girls. He and Stan returned to the apartment to drop off Roxanne's bag before Rich headed for the gym and Stan went to his firm's office on Madison Avenue.

That evening, since no one was interested in getting dressed up, Stan invited them to dinner at Smith and Wollensky's.

"We won't make reservations and take our chances sitting in the bar waiting for a table. If we can't get in there, we'll come back and try the Palm," he'd told them.

Rich hadn't been to either but had walked past both restaurants many times. Sitting in the lounge waiting for their table, after their second cocktail arrived, Rich, who was seated next to Roxanne, said, "Margaret tells me that you teach art."

Roxanne turned toward him. "Yes, that's right. I teach at St. Randolph's in Pawtucket."

"Do you do a lot of work with clay?"

"I do. Why do you ask?"

"Well, if you don't mind me saying, I was admiring your hands. They remind me of my junior high art teacher. She had beautiful, strong hands too. You could tell that she worked with them a lot. She did a lot of work with clay, especially with a pottery wheel. She sold things that she had made. You could tell she was doing something she really loved." He grinned sheepishly like he was telling a big secret. "And I admit to having a seventh-grade crush on her."

Roxanne smiled. "I work with the wheel. In fact, I love throwing pots, one of the things I really try to get my students involved in. I'd like to see an increased interest in pottery. It's the sort of thing that someone can hold onto—a lifelong pastime or diversion, or a way to relax."

"Besides, it's so sensual—you remember that scene from *Ghost*?" Stan added.

"Oh hush!" Rox said, giving him a playful pat on the arm. "Did you work with the pottery wheel in school?"

"I tried but could never get started. For some reason, I could never get the clay centered, and the few times that I did, the whole thing would collapse. My teacher told me that I was too impatient and worked too fast, but I think it was just my big, clumsy hands."

Roxanne took his hand in hers. "Why? You have beautiful hands. You'll have to make the trip up to Providence. I have a wheel at the house, and we can work on your technique."

"If you're going to work on his technique, I'm coming too," Margaret broke in, taking Rich's other hand in hers.

"What about me?" Stan asked.

"You can rent *Ghost*, sweetheart," Roxanne said with a loving smile, leaning across the table and placing the palm of her hand softly on his cheek. They all laughed. At the same time, she tightened her grip on Rich's hand.

Just as they finished their second drink, they were shown to their table. By the look on his face, everyone could tell that Rich was a little shocked when he looked at the menu.

Stan leaned across the table. "Don't worry about the prices. It's all on me. I'm on an expense account, and you saved my clients a bundle by letting me stay at your apartment, so they can spring for a nice dinner for all of us," he said with a wink.

"Yeah, but back home you could buy half a calf for the price of a steak in this place."

"Yes, that's true, but consider this—back home, you'd still be back home, and now you're eating steak in the big city with us," Stan joked with a big smile and another wink.

On Sunday afternoon, they walked with Roxanne and Stan to Grand Central for the two o'clock train and the return to Providence. As they waited on the platform, Roxanne took Rich aside.

"You'd better be good to her. Take care of her because if you hurt her in any way, Stan and I will hunt you down, and I will hurt you. This I swear." She looked him straight in the eyes and then gave him a kiss, hard on the lips. She turned and said her good-byes to Margaret as Stan and Rich made theirs.

"Have you told him?" Roxanne asked in a whisper.

"No, not yet," Margaret answered. "I don't think I can."

"Yes, you can. You have to—not for him, but for you. You have to be sure where your head is. You have to be sure about who you're getting involved—with whom he's getting himself involved."

After seeing them off, they walked back to the apartment. Margaret took Rich's arm, leaning close.

"Well, what do you think about Roxanne and Stan?"

"Well, Marvelous, they definitely are the odd couple. What is she, six inches taller than him? How did they get together? Why didn't you tell me she was African American?"

"Is she? I guess because it shouldn't matter."

"It doesn't, but I guess I didn't expect it. I hope it didn't show. What's their story?"

"Story? No story. Rox told me that they were in love in high school—and then she grew eight inches. It didn't mean anything to Stan. He used to say that he'd love her if she was three feet tall, but at more than six feet, there was so much more to love. I always thought that was sweet. Roxanne must have also!"

"Well, I think Stan breaks every stereotype of an accountant I might have ever had. I don't think I've ever seen anyone so intense but laid-back at the same time, and I don't think Roxanne likes me very much."

Margaret stopped walking, let go of his arm, and turned to face him.

"What makes you say that? I think she really warmed to you with those comments about her hands. In fact, she told me she thought I'd made a good choice asking you to share the apartment."

"So this is what this was? An inspection?"

"Well, sort of. The real one will come when you meet my sisters, but I love Roxanne and Stan and trust their judgment. Did you think it strange that neither of them asked a whole lot about you—personal questions? When you and Stan were talking the other night, did he ask you anything about Sandy or Arizona or anything like that?" She stopped speaking for a moment. "I've been telling them about you since the first time you walked into the Oyster Bar, and I trust their opinion of you … Let me rephrase that. I want you with me, and they—well, their opinion matters a great deal to me—that I've made the right decision about asking you to move into the apartment. Yes, in a way, I did need their approval—not their permission, but their gut feelings about you—the same as I must have had about you when I first laid eyes on you."

"Well, I'm glad they approve of me," Rich muttered under his breath. They walked in silence the rest of the way to the apartment. Rich couldn't figure out whether he was angry, and if so why. Was it anger or a feeling of betrayal, that he was the only one who was not "in on this little conspiracy." He kept rolling it around in his head and kept coming up empty. No, it wasn't anger—not really— but he could not shake the thought of what would have happened if Stan and Roxanne had given him a "thumbs down."

They stripped the linens off of the bed in the third bedroom, and Rich stuffed them in the washer. Margaret went to her room and closed the door.

Rich was tired, but he didn't want to take a nap. He turned on the television, turned down the volume, and watched but could not concentrate on the middle innings of a baseball game. He began flipping channels between baseball games and thought about taking a walk.

Something was simmering inside of him, and he didn't like it. He wasn't sure if he was hurt or angry or both. He wanted to say, "To hell with Stan and to hell with Roxanne." He was afraid that he couldn't stop before he said, "And to hell with you." At least, he thought, even if he didn't say it, that's what Margaret might hear—and he wasn't hurt or angry enough to risk that.

An hour later, Margaret came out of her room and went straight into the bathroom. He heard the water running, and a few minutes later she came, stood behind him for a moment, went to the refrigerator, and brought out a bottle of beer and one of seltzer.

She came and took her place on the sofa and sat in silence for a few minutes. He turned off the television.

"I have to … I want to tell you something." From the redness in her eyes, he thought she had been crying. He didn't say anything as he moved from the recliner to sit beside her on the sofa.

"Roxanne and Stan have been together for a long time, at least for as long as I've known them—way before that even. He used to come over to our dorm all the time. I liked Stan from the first time I met him. He was a lot of fun in a bumbling sort of way. He's always been good to Roxanne, and she's always been good to him. I think he spent more time at our place than his own. I don't know how they made it all the way through school without getting married. The wedding was the week after we graduated. I was her maid of honor." The tears started to fall. After a minute, she continued.

"During my sophomore year, I started seeing a guy—his name's not important. We were pretty steady—I thought it was steady. Once basketball season started, there wasn't a lot of time—maybe once a week, a couple of Saturday evenings a month. He wanted things to go much faster than I did and wasn't afraid to let me know that he could always walk out and find someone else."

She opened the seltzer and took a drink.

"At the end of February, he came over. Roxanne and Stan were out seeing a movie. He'd been drinking. I guess it was, or he thought it was some sort of ultimatum—sleep with him that night or he would break up with me. I asked him to leave—I told him to leave. I was getting scared."

She took another drink. Rich opened his beer.

"He hit—slapped me. It was hard. My nose and lip were bleeding. He grabbed me by the arm and pulled me out of my chair. He had me by the hair and was dragging me toward the bedroom. I was screaming and kicking, and he just laughed. Roxanne and Stan walked in just then."

Margaret had been looking at her hands, holding the bottle on her knees, and now looked up for the first time.

"Stan is a laid-back guy, but you should have seen him then. Rox told me that he went absolutely "ninja" on the guy. Roxanne pulled me away, put me in my bedroom, and then I guess that she went after him too.

"I honestly think she'd have killed him. Stan said that she went into the kitchen and came out with a skillet. Rox ended up actually sitting on the guy while Stan phoned the police. I was hysterical. After they took him away and took my statement, Stan and Roxanne took me to the hospital to be checked. Nothing was broken, but I had a cut lip, a black eye, and a deep bruise on my arm where he'd grabbed me.

"Sometime later the next week, I went to get my hair cut. I used to wear it long, about to the middle of my back, and I'd tie it in a ponytail during games. I've kept it short since then," she stammered as she absently ran a hand through her hair and took another drink of seltzer.

"He got six months, along with being thrown out of the university. Once he got out of jail—I don't even know how long he served—I had a restraining order on him until I left school. Since no one had actually seen him hit me, they couldn't do more than attempted this and attempted that, but Roxanne told me that Stan saw him one day and told him that if he ever saw him near me, he'd let Roxanne work him over with her frying pan."

She stopped and took a deep breath, wiping away the tears.

"So you see, when I told Rox that I was going to ask you to move in, she told me how happy she was for me and that she was going to come to the city and check you out. You wouldn't know it, but Stan and Rox spent the night here many times before you moved in, and you don't know that she's been down here two other times before this weekend. The first time, just to have lunch and get a look at you. The other time on one of our girls' nights out. She said that she wanted to see if you were as amazing as I described."

"She's been here while I was working the grill? You'd have thought I would have noticed her."

"Now, she wanted Stan to meet you too. They wanted to meet you and see how I was dealing with our being together. You're the first guy I've been close to since then. Stan went to the office for a little while yesterday afternoon but then met us at Barnes and Noble. The two of them had it all planned out, and the three of us had a long talk. They told me that they liked you and felt that you could be trusted—I know that trusted was the wrong word—but they were happy that I was happy. I know it sounds like they were auditioning you for a job, but that's not how it was."

Rich took a long drink of beer.

"I don't want you to think I needed them to approve you, but I did need them to feel comfortable that I'd made the right choice. I didn't want them to worry about me."

"You didn't tell me the guy's name, and I never want to know it—because if I ever run into him, Roxanne and her frying pan will be the least of his worries."

Margaret leaned toward him, put her arms around his neck, and held him tight. He returned the embrace and lifted her onto his lap and held her as she cried on his shoulder. Some of the tears that he was feeling were his.

"What a pair we make," she whispered.

"I'm sorry," he answered, holding her tighter. "I'm sorry for being an ass. I'm sorry for what happened, and I'm sorry that …" He couldn't finish as she buried her face deeper into his neck.

8

Rich and Margaret went out for dinner one night a week, usually on Saturday. Most of the time it was casual, but sometimes they decided to splurge and got dressed up. Research and development, they called it. It was never like Stan's extravagance. They saved those sorts of outings for the times when the four of them got together and "painted the town," as Roxanne liked to say.

On the other nights, they just threw something on the table, even though both of them were pretty good cooks. Most of the time, after flipping burgers all day, all either was interested in having in the evening was a peanut butter sandwich, a salad, or some sliced fruit.

At the end of October, Rich's supervisor invited the two of them to have dinner with his wife and him. He told Rich that they were going to the Metropolitan Club; it would be formal but not black tie.

As they dressed, Rich had a feeling that Margaret was nervous or apprehensive about something. She carried her coat out of her bedroom and laid it across the back of one of the chairs. It was a big, quilted, nylon coat that she'd purchased while she was at the university … a sort of long, down-filled parka. It was dark blue and was in good shape even though it was well worn. It was the coat that she usually wore when they were out on cold evenings.

She went back to her room and brought out another, lighter coat, not as long. It was cold outside, but they were going to take a cab to the Club, so the coat might have been warm enough.

Rich noticed what he thought was her indecision and picked up the first coat and placed it over her shoulders.

"This one is fine," he assured her.

"But it's so old and frumpy looking."

"No one will notice, and if anyone cares, it's on them—not you."

After they arrived, Rich quickly helped her out of her coat.

"You look beautiful. You are beautiful," he whispered before he checked it along with his. He hoped that she would relax.

They had a wonderful evening. Tom offered to order for them and made all the right choices.

Rich had admitted that, besides red and white, he did not know one wine from another.

They began with sautéed foie gras with figs. After he tasted it, Rich put his knife and fork on his plate and sat, staring at it. He took a deep breath and slowly let it out. It was almost a sigh.

"Something wrong?" asked Tom's wife, Jeanne.

It took a moment. Rich seemed to be in a daze.

"No, nothing," Rich replied. "I guess I've never had foie gras before. I've had goose liver but nothing like this. I think this is the most delicious thing I've ever tasted. If I had known you could do anything like this with goose liver, we would never have just fried or roasted them with the goose."

"Well, it's a little more than goose liver," Jeanne said with lightness in her voice.

"I'm glad you like it," Tom said. "It's one of the specialties here. I really look forward to coming here, just to have a chance to order it."

The rest of the meal was just as delicious—grilled salmon with some sort of lemon, wine, and herb sauce, along with mixed, steamed baby vegetables and a variety of desserts. Over their cognac, Tom asked if anyone was up to sitting in a piano bar somewhere. They all agreed that it would be a good idea and found themselves on Fifth Avenue waiting for a cab that would take them to the Terrace Lounge in the Waldorf-Astoria.

Margaret was thankful for the warmer coat as they waited. Once again, they checked their coats, and Rich noticed Jeanne's fur coat but did not say anything about it as he took Margaret's.

"If you don't mind me asking," Rich said to Tom on Monday morning, after thanking him for everything on Saturday evening, "what sort of fur coat was your wife wearing on Saturday evening?"

"I think she had on the nutria—it was black, and the fur was long, wasn't it? Wait a minute, you're not one of those activists who dumps paint on fur coats, are you?"

"No, no—in fact, I'm one of those people who may have sold someone else a pelt that was turned into a coat—and am now also hooked on foie gras and figs."

"Yeah, it was the nutria. She also has a sable coat."

"What's a nutria?"

"It's a sort of rat—a rodent—a big, very expensive rodent."

"I think they're all some sort of rodent, or weasel—some sort of varmint, at least, but I don't think I've ever heard of a nutria. It was a beautiful coat."

"Well hey, if you're thinking about buying one, or any other fur coat, check into a used one first. Don't look at new before you look at some used coats. You can find some good buys down on Seventh Avenue, below Thirty-Fourth Street."

"I need a new coat," Rich announced a few nights later. "Suede and shearling isn't going to cut it for me as an overcoat anymore. Will you come with me and help pick it out?"

"You don't think you can find a coat by yourself?"

"I'm not sure what I want, and I trust your opinion more than a salesman's."

"Okay, when do you want to go?"

"Tomorrow night. I'll skip the gym since I don't have class, and we can go right after we get cleaned up, unless you have other plans."

"No, that sounds good to me. It's a date!"

Rich didn't know where to start, so they stopped first at Macy's and made their way back Uptown. Finally after window shopping up Fifth Avenue, they made their way to Lexington and Bloomingdales.

They came in off the street and went down the stairs. The men's department was in the lower level; you could come in directly from the Fifty-Ninth Street subway station.

As he searched through the racks, a sales clerk approached. "Looking for something in particular?"

"I'm not sure. I need a coat, but I'm thinking it should be more of a raincoat than topcoat."

"Wool, maybe cashmere, but something durable—you know what I mean?" added Margaret.

The clerk showed him several styles and colors.

"The problem is," he noted, "I don't think that we're going to find a lot of things in the store that are long enough. We can order them, of course, but I don't think that most of the things we have will be quite right. We can try some things for size though." He showed them more dress coats.

Nothing seemed to catch their eye.

"What about a good trench coat?" the salesman suggested.

"I don't want to look like a spy."

"No, they're very stylish and come in several colors. They're durable, and some have a removable liner so you can wear them three seasons—but again, I'm not sure we would have the proper length. I'd hate to send you out in something that was too short."

"I like that one," Margaret said as the salesman helped Rich slip a coat over the suit jacket he was wearing.

It was a tan-colored Burberry, a traditional trench coat style.

"This is a coat that will last you a lifetime," the salesman said, stepping back. "It's the sort of coat that you can ball up and toss in the overhead compartment of a plane or train, and it'll still look good when you put it on. You wouldn't do that with a good cashmere coat—and it's still dressy enough to wear over a tux. It may certainly be the last coat that you'll ever buy, and it'll still be around for your children to fight over when you've gone."

"Did you hear that, dear?" Margaret said. "It'll be one more thing for the children to fight over when you're gone!"

"It fits you well across the shoulders. How does it feel across the chest? Put your arms up like this ... but, alas, it's too short—or at least it's not as long as I would want it to be. But that's certainly up to you."

"I think I'd want it longer, don't you, M? And I'm not sure that I'm crazy about tan," Rich said as he stood in front of the three panels of mirrors. "What do you think?"

"The important question is whether there's a possibility of getting a longer one."

"Alas, I'm terribly afraid that there isn't," the salesman said. "As much as I'd like to sell you this coat, I cannot honestly do it—it just wouldn't be right. What I would suggest," he lowered his voice to a conspiratorial whisper, "is that you go and have one custom made. It'll cost a little more than this one, but then you can have a wider choice of colors and linings. There are several places in Midtown ... one on Forty-Sixth Street around Fifth and another on Fifth between Forty-First and Forty-Second. They won't be open yet this evening, and I think you might actually have to make an appointment to be measured and fitted, and I understand that it takes a few weeks to have one specially made—but I don't know about this time of the year. I think it would be the wisest thing to do."

After thinking about it for a few minutes and discussing it with Margaret, Rich thanked the man for his time and honesty. As they approached the stairs, Rich stopped and took Margaret's arm.

"Okay, now it's your turn."

"My turn for what?"

"Let's go and find you a new coat."

"I don't need a new coat," Margaret protested.

"Yes, you do, and I'm going to buy it for you," he answered, steering her toward the stairs. "Women's coats?" he asked a clerk as they walked past.

"Ladies' outerwear is on the fourth floor," came the reply.

"Besides, I've got to get out of here. I think I'm feeling a little claustrophobic!"

"Are you okay?" Margaret asked as they got to the stairs. "Calm down, you look pale! Take a deep breath!"

"Did that guy really say alas?"

"Here, give me your coat. Are you okay? Do you want to sit down for a while?"

Rich still felt dizzy as he sat heavily on the stairs of Bloomington's lower level. "No, I'm fine. I don't know what it was, but suddenly that ceiling seemed so low, and it started to close in on me. I've never felt like that before." After sitting for a few minutes, they climbed the stairs to the main floor.

A salesperson approached them. "Good evening, my name is Maria. May I help you find something?"

"Yes, we'd like to see some coats," Rich answered. "How come my salesman didn't tell us his name?" he whispered to Margaret.

"No, we don't," Margaret cut in, pushing him away.

Rich smiled, excused himself, offered Margaret his arm, and they walked back toward the escalators, stopping and stepping to one side.

"Listen," Rich said, taking her hands in his. "Remember the other night when we had dinner with Tom and Jeanne? Do you remember how nervous and apprehensive you were? It was all because of your coat. I could see it. I'm right, aren't I?"

"It's just a coat."

"I know it's just a coat, M. A coat that you've had for what … ten years? If it makes you feel that way, it's time to get a new one, and I want to get it for you. Please, let me do this for you. I know there will be occasions coming up when we'll be out with people—your friends, my friends, it doesn't matter. What will you do the next time Stan and Roxanne come down, and she shows up with her mink?

"M, as far as I'm concerned, you're the most beautiful woman in the room—any room—and I don't want you to feel any other way, just because the coat you wore to the party is old. Please, let me do this for you. Do you know how much that Burberry would have cost me? I didn't even flinch. You know that we get a big chunk of a bonus at the end of the year, and this is how I want to spend it."

Margaret's eyes began to fill with tears. She put her arms around his chest and hugged him with her head on his shoulder.

"I don't need a new coat," she whispered.

"I know you don't. So, do you want to start with the furs or look at something else first? Hey, how about a trench coat? Then we could look like twin spies, and our kids will have something else to fight over when we're gone!"

Margaret smiled as she stepped back from him, looking into his eyes. "Okay, let's look—look, but no furs! I think that strange feeling you had downstairs affected your brain!"

9

One evening in February, Rich took his laundry out of the dryer. When he got back to his bedroom, he found a blue bikini swimsuit. He figured that Margaret had misplaced a pair of her underwear before he realized what size it was, what it actually was, and how it had gotten into the dryer; Margaret had put it there while he was in the shower. She'd waited three days for the chance to catch him doing his laundry. Without giving it anymore thought, he hung it on the doorknob of her bedroom.

When she'd finished her shower and come into the kitchen, she asked him about it, twirling the underwear on her finger. Then she said, "These aren't mine. They're for you."

"What are what? Oh, those," he answered as he looked up from his book.

"You're supposed to wear them."

"I'm supposed to wear them where? And when?"

"Neil called and told me that they need you to shave your chest and back—down to a bikini."

"I'm supposed to do what?"

"Oh, come on. They want you to do a shoot, and the guy whose head they're using has a bare chest and back."

"They're going to use my body for pictures of some athlete? A swimmer? What's wrong with his body?"

"Something about a tattoo that will conflict with an endorsement—and I don't especially think he's a swimmer."

Rich looked at her. "You're kidding, right?

"No, I'm not kidding. I hear the guy's got a tattoo. Look, it's a thousand dollars, and they want you to shave down. They want you—well, they want your torso. Neil tried to airbrush the hair out, but it erased your six-pack and the muscles in your chest and biceps."

He rubbed his hand over the hair on his chest. "I've always thought this was one of the reasons Neil used me. I'm not one of those guys that shaves his legs and arms and goodness knows what else—they said they use me because I look like a normal person." He looked down at his chest and stomach. "I never pictured myself as especially simian-like."

"What like?"

"Simian, you know, like some sort of monkey."

Rich still had a look of disbelief on his face as she turned and walked out of the kitchen. He got up from the table and went to his room with the swimming suit bunched in his fist.

Margaret knocked on his door a few minutes later. When he opened it, she was holding a small wet-dry trimmer and a package of high-end disposable razors. "If you put them on in the shower, I'll come in and shave your back for you."

"My back? Am I some sort of gorilla? Tell me. I'm strong—I can take it," he joked. "How's this? Do they make me look fat?"

Margaret exploded in laughter. He was wearing the bikini over a pair of long, baggy swimming trunks. "Monica, is that you? See, that's what I mean about the ad. Who else would you expect to find? And don't come near me with those disposables. I'll use my razor, thank you very much!"

"The ad works because the guy can't believe how good Monica looks in those panties—just like this will work because no one would believe how good you look in those—except me."

Standing in the shower, wearing the two pairs of shorts, he trimmed the hair on his chest and stomach. When Margaret heard him shut off the clippers, she stepped out of her slippers and stepped into the shower. Her sweatpants and T-shirt looked just as out of place as his swimwear. She took the trimmer from him and began to trim the hair on the back of his neck, between his shoulder blades, and in the middle of the small of his back as he leaned against the wall, "assuming the position." When she finished, she stepped back out. He turned on the water and stood under the shower. Then, after replacing the blade, he used his razor on his chest and stomach. When he finished and turned off the water, Margaret stepped back into the shower. Rich handed the razor to her, and she began shaving the areas that she had just trimmed.

"This is heavy," she noted, bouncing the razor in her palm. "How long have you had this?"

"Since eighth grade, when I started shaving. They don't make the handle anymore, but you can still buy the blades. They keep coming out with something new, but I like that one."

"You know, people will talk," she whispered as she continued to shave. "We're in the shower together again. 'I'm sorry, Margaret can't come to the phone right now; she's in the shower with Rich!'"

"Very funny. Hey, what are you doing back there? Let's not overdo this!"

Margaret pulled the waistbands of both swimming suits down as she moved the razor down and then across his lower back. "The whole idea of using this bikini is to know how much to shave. Now stop being such a crybaby and—well—just shut up and enjoy it."

"Can we call this thing something besides a bikini? Isn't there another name for it? The hair will grow back, won't it?"

"There. Finished. Now turn around and let me check your front. Smooth as a baby's bottom," she commented, running her hand across his chest and stomach.

"Baby's butt—is that the look they're after? Or are they looking for one of those anorexic, skinny, junkie-looking types? Whose head are they using?"

She leaned in and whispered, "Let me fill you in on a little secret. You could never be mistaken for anyone but the stud you are." She playfully nibbled his earlobe with her hand just above the waistband of his shorts.

"Okay, okay, let's not get carried away and start something we can't finish." He placed his arms across his chest, mockingly protecting his modesty, laughing.

"I wish I'd taken a before and after picture … especially of you in that getup."

"No pictures! I'm going to have to figure out some way to keep my face out of the ones Neil's going to take. I can just see them showing up on some Internet site. Who's Who at Arizona State. What will the guys at the club say?"

"The thing is that you don't look like a normal person. You look like a guy who takes good care of himself and cares about his body. Neil knows that, but for this one time he needs you to do this—to look like those other guys."

Rich thought he would die of embarrassment during the shoot that next afternoon. Since his head was going to be replaced with another, he pulled out a pair of plastic eyeglasses with a fake nose and mustache from his bag.

"What are those for?" Neil asked.

"Protection. This way, if some of these pictures get out, I'm still safe. And none of these pictures will get out, will they, Neil?"

Neil laughed. "I guarantee that none of the pictures of your head connected to your body will get out of my lab. If you want to wear those glasses, go right ahead. It doesn't matter an inch with me; it's not your face we're after."

The shoot was over quickly, and he was thankful to have a chance to get out of the skimpy swimming suit and back into his jeans. Neil was happy with the way the pictures looked and said that he was sure that the clients, something to do with a shoe company, would also be happy with the way things turned out.

Through it all, Rich could not understand the connection between an athletic shoe company and the blue bikini.

10

They usually did especially well on days when there was a workday parade, like Columbus or St. Patrick's Day. Margaret wasn't sure whether it was their proximity to the fire station down the street or their location in Midtown, but from midday on, they were always crowded. After her first St. Patrick's Day at the Firehouse, she decided to stay open longer. It turned out to be a good plan. The bars were all crowded, but there were many families looking for a place for a quick lunch apart from all of the heavy drinking and revelry.

This March 17 dawned very cold. It had rained the day before, but the morning was clear. It would be a good day for a parade. The city began filling early as people poured out of the trains and subways. Who knew how many of them actually got to Fifth Avenue and watched the parade. It sure seemed like most of them were just in the city to enjoy the atmosphere of what might have been the biggest one-day party in America.

Twice while walking back from the office, Rich stopped to ask if someone needed help finding their way. It was easy to recognize a tourist, especially when they were scouring over a map. He figured anyone who looked as he must have looked when he first arrived in the city definitely needed some help. One particular guy didn't have a map, but by his look of bewilderment, Rich could tell that neither he nor the three people with him had a clue as to where they were or where they were going.

"Yeah, we're looking for a burger and a beer," the guy answered.

"I know just the place. It's a few blocks from here."

They struck up a conversation while they walked, and by the time they arrived at the Firehouse, Rich thought he knew everything there was to know about the man, his wife, son, and daughter-in-law.

As it turned out, Mike Halligan knew New York. He admitted that he was just a little confused that morning.

"I knew we didn't want to try to cross Madison or Fifth Avenue, but I wasn't sure whether we should go Up or Downtown."

"You'd think we were a bunch of foreigners or something," his son, Christopher, added.

"We've only lived in some part of the city all our lives!"

"And of course neither of them would ask for directions or ideas," Kathy, Mike's wife, joined in, giving her husband a nudge as they walked arm in arm.

They continued walking and talking until they turned the corner onto Fortieth Street and saw the crowd standing on the sidewalk.

"Oh no, it looks like I'm going to be late for work," Rich said as he picked up the pace.

"What do you mean? It looks like we're all going to be late if this is the place you're taking us," Mike answered.

"No, you don't understand. I work here. I'm the guy that's not only going to buy you lunch, but I'm supposed to be cooking it."

"So, you're a shill for this place," Chris's wife, Patty, said with a laugh. "At least you weren't wearing one of those sandwich boards up and down the street."

"A shill? Well, I guess I am sort of—and don't think we haven't thought of the sandwich board—but not only am a shill, I'm a part owner too." Rich led them to the door, excusing himself. He went straight to the grill without taking the time to change his clothes, just putting his coat, tie, and jacket on top of one of the coolers.

The Halligans appeared to genuinely enjoy themselves, along with everyone else. The place was loud and crowded and warm—a welcome change from the cold, loud, and crowded streets.

After that, Mike made it a point to stop in at least twice a month, having regained his bearings and sense of direction. They'd see him and sometimes Kathy, but he was usually with Christopher. They counted them among their regular customers, which Mike thought was a great compliment, especially when they all called him by name, as they did with many of their customers.

Somewhere along the way, Mike must have heard Margaret and Rich talking about their upcoming plans and invited them to come and spend the weekend with him and Kathy at their house in Montauk.

"It's right on the water. You can come and go as you please, and we'd love to have you both for a day or the whole weekend."

They gladly accepted, and that was their introduction to Montauk and the east end of Long Island. On Sunday afternoon, after a pleasant and restful weekend, and as they prepared to return to the city, Kathy invited them to use the house whenever they could get away.

"During the summer, we're out here only a couple of weekends a month, and Chris and Patty have a place on the Jersey Shore, so they don't use it, and we'd be happy to have someone in and out of here so the place gets used. During the winter, we're hardly ever here anymore, even though it's a great time to be out of the city. We keep the place heated all winter, so it might as well be used."

Mike agreed, and the deal was sealed. He would always remind them of the opportunity when he came in for lunch. Margaret and Rich were happy to accept the invitation, and Mike and Kathy were always happy to give them use of the house.

11

"I'm going out to Home Depot. You wanna come?" Rich said to Margaret.

"Now why on earth would I want to go out to Home Depot?" She looked at the clock as she stepped out of her shoes. They'd taken a long walk home from their favorite Chinese restaurant. "It's nine o'clock!"

"They're open all night. Come on, it'll be fun. Home Depot's like the palace of things you need. Going to the one in Cheyenne is like a pilgrimage. Dad still looks forward to it like a kid waiting for Christmas. Everyone back home does. That's one of the things he always likes to do when I come home."

"No, watching you eat rice with chopsticks is fun. Riding the Seven Train out to Queens at ten o'clock on a Saturday night is not my idea of fun."

"Suit yourself, but you're going to miss out on a great time."

The next morning when they returned from church and brunch, she saw the box sitting next to the table. She hadn't heard him come in after his trek to Queens, and she couldn't figure out how she'd missed the box when they left the apartment earlier.

"You're one of the strangest people I've ever met," she said.

"Why? What makes you say that?"

"What are you going to do with a barbecue grill?"

"Grill stuff. The next time Roxanne and Stan come down, we can grill something and have dinner here."

"We have a grill downstairs."

"That's not the same. This one's for the roof."

"You'll never get it up those spiral stairs. Besides, Stan loves to eat out. He loves to bill his expense account for dinner. He could also be putting a two-hundred-dollar-a-night hotel charge on it instead of staying here. It's almost like—well, it's like he wants to dare someone in the office to challenge him about it. He's saving them money in the long run, and Roxanne likes the chance to get dressed up once in a while."

"Actually, the reason I went out there was to get this," he said, holding up a long-handled shovel. "The grill was on sale."

"And what are you going to do with a shovel? Don't tell me—you're going to dig a hole?"

"You bet!"

Margaret couldn't remember seeing him so excited. "If you really loved and cared about me, you would have brought home an ice-cream maker."

"I can always go back. They're open twenty-four-seven."

"Don't you dare. I'd gain twenty pounds! And where are you going to dig this hole?"

"On the beach—today. I'm going to take it to the beach and dig a hole. I just feel like digging a hole. Is that so strange? It's good exercise. Why? Do you think that's strange?"

"Oh, no particular reason. Tell you what, you can take that to the beach, but we won't sit together on the subway."

"Well, if you're embarrassed about being seen with a guy carrying a shovel—well, I guess you'll just have to sit by yourself then. But you think I'm strange? You should see some of the characters on the Seven Train out of Queens at midnight on a Saturday night."

"What—like a guy carrying a shovel and a barbecue grill? I don't know, but that's pretty strange in my book. How'd you do that anyway?"

"Well, you should have come along. Even with the grill and the shovel, I wouldn't have placed in the top ten of weird—and it was only midnight. I'm sure the night was still young."

Margaret remembered the night they had set off for Queens to purchase the pair of screen doors for the little terrace. Rich carried them back to the subway, and during the ride back to Manhattan, she held one, and he held the other, sitting across from each other, talking through the screens. What a sight that must have been!

As they headed toward Coney Island, the subway cars were so crowded no one noticed or seemed to notice the guy wearing shorts, an athletic shirt, backpack, and cowboy boots, carrying a long-handled shovel.

"Where did you get those?" Margaret asked, pointing to his boots.

He looked at his feet. "I wear these every day at the grill."

"Well, I guess this is the first time I've seen you wearing them with shorts, and I've never noticed them. I can't say that I think the look will ever catch on. And I guess I've never noticed how hairy your legs are."

"How many times have you seen my legs? Just goes to show how much you pay attention—and my legs have always been this hairy!" He noticed a lady sitting near enough to hear them give his legs a long look.

"I guess it must be the boots."

"That's me, always trying to make a fashion statement—right on the cutting edge!"

As he stood holding the vertical handrail on the subway with one hand and the shovel with the other, several people grabbed the handle, as if it was another handrail.

When they arrived at the beach on Coney Island, they walked along the boardwalk a hundred yards past the fishing pier. There weren't many people around there. The sun was blinding, and the sand was hot.

"This looks like a good spot. Do you want to go somewhere else or do you want to lie here?"

"Oh, this is fine. I want to lie right here and watch. This might be the best show on the beach. How big a hole you think you're going to dig?"

"I don't know. Till I'm tired, I guess."

With one hand, he dug a small hole in the sand and buried the plastic bag that carried their IDs and subway passes.

She took the blanket out of the backpack he was carrying and spread it on the sand over the hole that he'd finished covering. He took the pack off of his shoulders and laid it and its contents, including a radio and a gallon jug of tea, on the blanket as she sat and took off her shoes and shirt and stepped out of her shorts, revealing a string bikini.

"Wow! I don't have to worry about anyone staring at me. No, sir!"

Margaret looked up at him. "Thanks, I knew you'd like it!"

Rich put on a pair of leather work gloves and prepared to dig.

"You know, you're going to have white hands and calves when you're finished," she warned as she tuned the radio to a baseball game. "Come over here and at least let me put some of this sunscreen on your shoulders."

"Okay, but I plan to sweat it off real fast," he said, taking a big drink of iced tea as he knelt beside her.

"There you go, digger boy. Now get to work—hey, I like that—Digger Reiley—it fits! 'Luke, I want all that sand out of Boss Paul's hole before the end of the game!' Where you going to start? Don't dig too close, so that people don't automatically suspect that we're together, but don't go too far away. I want to keep an eye on you."

Rich tied a faded blue bandana around his forehead, stretched his back and legs a couple of times, picked up the shovel, and moved about ten feet farther down the beach.

"How's this?"

"A little to the left. That's perfect."

After about an hour, he was waist deep in an almost five foot by five foot, square hole, measured by the length of the shovel. He figured another hour and he'd be up to his chest and that would be deep enough.

Through the course of the afternoon, a number of people walked by and made it a point to look into the hole, curious as to what was going on. Some stopped to chat, but most just walked past.

A police officer rode her four-wheeled ATV over, shut off the engine, and climbed off.

"Digging a hole, I see."

"Yes, ma'am, I'm digging a hole."

"And I guess you're going to fill it back in before you leave?"

"Yes, ma'am, that's what I intended to do, unless you want me to leave it for some reason?"

"No, no, I'd like you to fill it back up. I wouldn't go too deep. I sure would hate to have it cave in on you. We'd have to tie a rope around your head and drag you out, and you'd probably lose a perfectly good shovel."

"I never thought of that, but I'll be careful."

"And when you fill it in, would you make sure that you pack it down pretty good as you go so we don't have any soft spots?"

"Yes, I will certainly do that, Officer."

"Well, then you have a nice day."

"Thank you, Officer. I will certainly do that also."

She got back on the ATV. "By the way, I've got to ask. Why are you digging a hole out here?"

"For the exercise," Rich answered.

She thought for a second. "Makes about as much sense as running a marathon, I guess." She rode away.

Rick climbed out of the hole, walked over to the blanket, and took a drink from the jug of iced tea. All of the ice had melted long ago.

"*Yes, ma'am, I certainly will, Officer—digging a hole I see, and you'd probably lose a perfectly good shovel.* Oh brother! Talk about shovel!" Margaret said, looking up and shading her eyes with her hand.

"I thought you were asleep."

"I was—until one of New York's finest rode up. You really think she came over to see what you were doing? I say she came over to check you out."

"With a babe laying right here?"

"You bet. She saw you from the boardwalk. She could see you were digging a hole. What'd she think you were doing? And she came over to get a better look. And I'm sure she got what she came for."

"I could've been burying a body, I guess. You really think she came all the way over here to get a closer look at me?"

"I know because it's exactly what I would have done!"

Rich flexed his arms as he peeled off his gloves and thumped his chest.

"Stop doing that or you'll have her coming back here."

"You know, she was almost my kind of woman. I could really go for someone packing heat—but …"

"But what?"

"Those black crew socks."

"That's her uniform."

"I know, but it was such a turn off. Even with the gun, I wouldn't be able to get past her wearing those black crew socks with shorts."

"Packing heat? I'll give you packing heat—I got your packing heat right here, fella! And black crew socks? I don't own a pair. Never have, never will!"

"Where's that sunscreen?"

"In the bag," she said, and turned onto her stomach and untied the strings on her bikini. He knelt beside her and rubbed the lotion on her back, shoulders, and legs.

"You're getting pretty good at that."

"But now I've got to get this stuff off my hands." He wiped the front and back of his hands on the back of his neck and shoulders and went back to his digging.

The game was in the eighth inning, and the hole had reached the desired depth of almost chest deep. Rich was just getting ready to climb out when three small boys, all about the same age, walked up to the edge.

"Are you looking for buried treasure?"

"Hey, mister, how you gonna get out of there?"

Rich looked around like he suddenly hadn't thought of that.

"That's what I've been trying to figure out. I thought I'd dig myself out, but it kept getting deeper and deeper!"

One of them got down on his hands and knees and peered in. "Wow, that's a deep hole! How long you been digging it?"

"Since the first inning of the Mets' game."

"The Mets stink. We like the Yankees!" another said, and the other two agreed with him.

"Can we play on the pile?" the third boy asked, pointing to the contents of the hole, now deposited next to it.

"Well, that would be okay, but I've got to start putting it all back in here."

"You mean you're just going to fill it up again?"

"I have to. That police lady that was here a little while ago told me I had to."

"Can we climb in there?"

"How old are you?"

"I'm six."

"I'm seven."

"I'm six."

"Where are your parents?"

"My parents are over there," one of the six-year-olds answered, pointing. "These guys are my cousins. They came with us."

"Well, all three of you go and ask if it would be all right, and I'll let you climb down. Only if they say it's okay." All three ran off.

A minute later, they were back. "My dad said it was okay, but only if you leave us in there."

"And they're supposed to remember to thank you," said the father of the six-year-old as he strolled over.

Rich tossed the shovel onto the beach, took the boys one by one, and lowered them into the hole, which was almost twice as deep as they were tall. When he got the third one in, he hoisted himself up and out, and looking down on the three, he rubbed the sand from his gloves.

"Hey, look," he called to the boy's father, who was approaching, "I caught me three more Yankees fans. Now I can bury them along with the three I caught yesterday."

"Go ahead!" the dad answered with a laugh.

"No! No you won't!" the three yelled in chorus.

"Bernie," the father introduced himself, extending his hand, "and that's my boy, Frank, and the other two are Tim and Paul, my sister's kids."

Pulling off his glove and shaking hands, he said, "I'm Rich, and that's Margaret."

"Did that police woman ask what you were doing?"

"Yeah, and she wanted to make sure I was planning to fill it back in."

"She was checking you out—a lot of girls, my wife included, have been keeping a close watch on you. I could tell she was disappointed as the hole got deeper and there was less of you to see," Bernie said with a laugh.

He jumped back into the hole. "Hey, that's just what my girlfriend said," Rich answered. "Okay, everybody out!" One by one, he lifted the three boys over the edge. "I've got to get back to work."

"Thanks," all three said, and they ran toward the surf as he climbed back out.

"We've been watching you all afternoon. You're pretty good with that shovel. Construction?"

"No, finance—bonds—but I've dug a few holes."

"I'm a bus driver."

"Oh yeah? Which route—or do you have regular routes?"

"I have the M-60 out of Queens, from La Guardia crosstown."

"Yeah, I know that one. I—we take it out to the airport and back, from 125th Street and Lexington."

"That's the one," Bernie answered, looking into the hole. "Find Jimmy Hoffa down there?"

"No, and I was surprised that I didn't find very much junk. One good-sized rock and a couple of bottles. I'm sure there was some broken glass but not much more than sand. A lot of sea glass. I'd be curious how old it was—I hit a layer of clay and decided that was deep enough. If I were an anthropologist, I would want to know about dinosaur bones."

"You mean paleontologist."

"Paleo what?"

"Paleontologist, they're the ones that study dinosaurs. You've never been to the Museum of Natural History?"

"No, must have missed that one—I'm not much for museums."

"Well, it's worth the trip. How long you been in New York—if you don't mind my asking?"

The three boys were back, climbing on the sand pile.

"Be careful there, guys. If you slide down this side, you'll fall all the way down that hole, and I may just have Rich leave you in there this time."

"Are you really going to fill it back up?" one of the boys asked.

"I have to. That's the deal with the police lady."

"Are you going to do it now or are you going to dig some more?" another boy asked.

"I'm going to fill it now. You see my pretty girlfriend lying over there? She's gonna want to go home pretty soon, and so I have to get this finished. But you guys can help. I'll fill it partway, and then you can come over and help me pack the sand down."

"Okay. We'll watch," said the seven-year-old.

When Rich had shoveled half the sand back into the hole, he jumped in and lowered all three boys in with him. They were still in over their heads.

"Okay, we need to jump around and make sure the sand is in good and tight."

All four started tramping down the soft sand, with the three boys jumping and dancing, packing the sand hard.

"Okay, that's good. All finished. Thanks, guys." He lifted the three out, and they ran back to the surf as he finished filling the hole.

It was a lot easier to fill the hole than it was to empty it. It took him less than an hour to shovel all of the sand back in, packing it down as he went. Finally the only evidence there was of a hole was the color of the sand that had been disturbed.

Rich laid the shovel next to the blanket, took off his gloves, boots, and socks, walked into the surf, and dunked himself a couple of times. He was there only for a few minutes when Margaret joined him in the waist-deep water.

"And he's good with kids—that means he's a real keeper!"

"They were cute. Darn!" Rich said.

"Darn what?"

"Darn, I thought you were sleeping. I've always wanted to come up to a girl on the beach and drop something cold on her back to see if she would jump up so I could see her breasts."

"Breasts? Do you have this death wish often? Besides, you've seen them already, remember?"

"That's not the same. I wanted to conduct a real scientific experiment—sort of like flushing all the toilets while someone's in the shower—and you ruined it for me. A lifetime of dreaming, and you shot it to pieces!"

"I keep telling you that was an accident!"

"The first two times maybe. And a little boy's dreams dashed all at once!"

"Sorry! You finished digging or are you planning some other excavations?"

"Finished for today. And I think I may have overdone it. I'm going to be sore tomorrow."

"Well, serves you right. If you would come to the beach and sit like a normal human being, you wouldn't have those problems. You're not a kid anymore."

"I know it, and I think I'm really going to regret it tomorrow. So are you. It looks like you maybe got too much sun. But you know what? I can't wait to come back and dig me another hole. You want me to get you a shovel so you can dig one too?"

"No thanks. The excitement would be too much for me. Why, I do declare, can you imagine these hands touching a shovel, or any other implement—not to mention the blisters? Well, people would think I was some sort of farmhand. Not the sort of thing a proper lady would do, most certainly! The shame would be just too much for my family to bear, and my reputation would be ruined for good!" she said with a drawl. "And did you really mean what you said to those kids?"

"What'd I say?"

"That I'm your pretty girlfriend."

"Well, you are pretty, and you'd never pass for a boyfriend."

"I'm your pretty girlfriend. I didn't think I'd ever hear you say that!"

He gave her a hug.

"Does that mean you'll sit next to me on the subway?"

"It's a deal."

"Will you hold the shovel?"

"No, that's not part of the deal."

On the way back to Manhattan, with his foot on the blade and the shovel handle resting against his shoulder, Rich fell asleep with his head on her shoulder. His back was so sore on Monday morning he didn't think he could get out of bed, but he was back on the beach the following Saturday afternoon, and the one after that, digging more holes.

12

Now in their second summer in the Firehouse, they decided they would close on Friday during July and August. Things really slowed down after lunch on Thursdays—Midtown Manhattan emptying for the weekend. Margaret had long ago hired a professional cleaning crew to come in on Thursday afternoons to give the place a good going-over, making everything ready for Monday. During the times of year they were open five days a week, the cleaning crew arrived on Friday afternoon.

On the first Thursday in June, Margaret was just getting ready to fire up the grill when Rich walked in, his arms full of packages.

"Do you know where my next bikini shoot is going to be?" he whispered.

"I didn't know there was a next. Neil didn't say anything about it, but that's not unusual. He must have been really happy with the pictures. Where's it going to be?"

"Jamaica—at some resort. Do you have a passport? Because you're coming along."

Margaret stared at him, stunned, putting down the grill brush that she had been using to adjust the grates.

"Jamaica! When?"

"Third week in July, which means that I—we—if you don't have one, have to go today down to the passport office and," he lowered his voice so that Steve couldn't hear, "once we get there, you'll have to shave me again—because I'm not going to let the girl that works for Neil do it."

"Oh, Lori's okay, and you know how much I look forward to getting you in the shower again."

"Do what again?" Steve asked.

"Nothing," Rich and Margaret answered at once.

"Nothing? Ain't I a part of this operation?" Steve asked.

"Yes, but only a very small part. Now let's get to work."

"Where's the passport office? How late are they open?" Margaret asked.

"Downtown somewhere, and I think we can make it down there this afternoon."

"Where we going?" Pam asked.

"We're going to Jamaica," Margaret answered, almost giggling.

Six weeks later, on a Friday morning, just a few minutes past ten thirty, they touched down in Montego Bay.

"Ah … July in Jamaica. Who thought this up? Could it be hotter?" Rich asked as they climbed down the stairs and walked across the tarmac toward the terminal. It wasn't actually that hot, but the humidity was like a wall.

"It was the resort's idea," Neil responded as he wiped his brow. "At least we'll have the place nearly to ourselves, which will make things a whole lot easier."

They cleared immigration and collected their bags. After clearing customs, they bundled out to the van that the resort had sent. The whole crew would be spending three days and two nights in the all-inclusive resort that was desperately trying to change its image from glitz and glamour to a place that also catered to ordinary people and families. They had already successfully started to attract the spring break crowds. Now, just as the cruise lines had done, they were going back after the young couples who were looking for a quiet place to spend a few days in the sun.

"This isn't one of those places where everyone walks around naked, is it?" Sam, one of the technicians, asked as they pulled through the gates.

"I hope not. I'm not really up to seeing a lot of fat, hairy tourists naked or in their bikinis," Margaret said, with a noticeable shiver.

"Or their fat, hairy husbands in their bikinis," added Neil. Everyone laughed.

"Now this is a fine time to worry about nudity," Lori scolded.

"Actually, there is another resort, just up the way. We passed it a few minutes ago," answered the driver. "They allow—or should I say encourage—nudity or even expect it. In fact, most of the time, everyone is naked. Some days they have different activities like midnight naked volleyball. Here, you might see someone go topless, though."

"Too much information," Sam said, holding up his hands in surrender.

"Why, Sam," Lori said teasingly, "I think you're blushing. I for one would love to have a shoot on a nude resort. It would give me a chance to hone all of my artistic skills with makeup."

"I'm with Sam on that one, Lori," Rich joked. "Way, way, way too much information!" Everyone laughed again.

Their room opened onto a terrace that looked out toward the turquoise and sapphire sea … colors Rich had never seen before. Huge clouds were building far out on the horizon.

"Come look at this. I think I could live here. This is going to be a spectacular day."

Margaret came out onto the balcony and leaned against him, stepping into the bright sunshine. She put her arm around his waist, and he did the same around hers.

"I've heard people talking about the color of the water down here, but you have to actually see it to understand what that means. What is that—lapis, azure?"

"Turquoise and dark turquoise if there is such a thing. Rox would know. Do you know you've got a gray hair?"

"We've got this view, and you're looking at me?" He turned to look at her. "I've got lots of hairs turning gray. Here, look at my arms."

"No, you've got lots of gray hairs on your head," Margaret said, taking hold of his chin and moving his head from side to side. "Your sideburns are really gray. You seem to deal with it just fine. When I find my first one, I'm gonna step in front of a bus. Is that why you keep your hair so short?"

"Actually, I like to say it's silver—or how about platinum blond—and no, I keep it short because it gets wavy when it's longer—and I suppose you see the gray hair because the sun is bright, and they stand out against my tan."

Margaret stepped back and looked at him in surprise. "You have wavy hair?" She ran her hand over the top of his head.

"I have very wavy hair. I keep it short because I don't want to worry about it. The way it is now, I can comb it in the morning, and it stays that way all day. When I wore it longer, I had to put something on it and keep messing with it all the time. If I go longer than a month without a haircut, the back curls and my sideburns get bushy—it drives me nuts."

"But girls love guys with wavy hair."

"That's the other reason I keep it short. I got tired of fighting off the chicks all day!"

"Well, my wavy-haired love, you're certainly full of surprises!" She hugged him and turned back toward the ocean.

"This is nice. Too bad it's only for two days—and in July. We should make plans to come down here sometime after the holidays and before spring break."

"How about Presidents' Day weekend? I wonder what the weather is like down here then."

"Are you serious? I'd love to," she answered, giving him a squeeze. "We have to get moving. Neil wants you down at the pool right away. They'll probably want to get a lot done this afternoon before those clouds roll in. Do you think they're headed this way? Which swimming suit are you going to wear?"

"You know which ones I don't want to wear—and no, the guy that brought up the bags said they don't expect any rain. It's not quite monsoon season yet. If they want to put together a spread for 'regular people,' why do they want me in such an irregular suit?"

"It's not irregular. A lot of guys wear those kinds of swimsuits, and you're not a regular guy. If they can pull it off, I think they all should—I think that's the point—and those are the type of guys they're after," Margaret explained as she opened her suitcase and then his.

Rich didn't seem to understand. Margaret thought it better that he didn't—at least for now.

"Here, take the yellow one, and if Neil wants you to change, you can. Are you going to shoot all day like that and then shave tonight?"

"Yeah, that's the plan. Neil told me he wanted me with hair on my chest today, and bare tomorrow. This is all getting too weird. I think I'll put the yellow one on underneath my blue one. That way, if they want me to change, I can just peel one off. And you put on plenty of sunscreen. I'm not going to spend the weekend with you suffering second-degree burns and the next two weeks peeling."

"Oh, don't worry, I'll use plenty. I don't think you can put both suits on at once. There isn't enough of one to hide the other. You'd better just carry the second one. I, however, want to get a little sun, but I'm planning to spend the better part of the day under an umbrella while someone serves me drinks. Be nice so all of this is over in a hurry and you can join me."

"No argument there. The quicker I can finish and get out of this suit is fine by me. They want some other shots later anyway, so we should have part of the afternoon free before we start again. Do you want to do anything special tonight?"

She looked up, and he caught himself.

"I mean for dinner."

"I know what you meant, and yes, I would like to do something special. After all, I *am* in Jamaica with a great guy with wavy hair!"

He gave her a puzzled look before heading to the bathroom, carrying the two swimming suits and his long, baggy shorts.

They didn't have that many out-of-town shoots, and when they did, Margaret always came along with Rich, while he almost never accompanied her. On those occasions, they stipulated that they have a double room with twin beds. Usually they paid the extra room expense out of pocket. Oftentimes they just happened to have twin beds already. At first the company thought it odd, but after awhile, no one gave it a second thought. Of course this added to the rumors that at least one of them was gay.

After three hours, the crew took a break. Rich couldn't remember how many times he'd changed clothes and swimming suits. He wrapped a towel around his waist and walked over to the edge of the sand, looking for Margaret. She was lying on her stomach at the far end of the pool terrace. He sat on the side of her lounge chair, picked up the bottle of sunscreen, and began to rub the lotion on her shoulders and back. She was wearing a bronze-colored, open-back, one-piece bathing suit and had slipped out of the straps. Rich continued smoothing the lotion on her arms.

"I'll give you an hour to cut that out." She sighed, her eyes closed.

"You're going to have to move pretty soon. The sun is going to move behind those trees," he said as he moved to the back of her legs.

"Oh, Rich, it's you!"

"No, it's the cabana boy, just checking up on all the guests."

"Well, while you're up, cabana boy, would you please get me another fruit punch or maybe a diet soda with lots of ice?"

"Yes, madam. Is there anything else you might desire?"

"There is. Hurry up and finish and get you and that hot swimming suit over here."

"Never! I'm not that sort of cabana boy. I'll rub lotion on your back, but I will not be your toy. I'll be back when I can, but it will be in my baggy trunks, and that's all you'll get."

"Which one are you in now—the yellow or blue one? I like that blue one."

"Don't ask."

"Which one? I want to see."

"No, no you can't."

"Oh come on, let me see." She pulled on the towel, revealing a red thong. She gasped, putting her hand over her mouth. "Monica, is that you?"

Rich dropped the towel, stood, and turned around slowly, holding his arms straight out.

"Have you ever seen such a thing? I will never understand how or why a guy would ever wear something like this. What I really can't figure out is—well, first, I can't figure out why someone would wear something like this—but how do they get away with it? I mean, if I wore a jockstrap on the beach, I'd be arrested, but this is little more than that. In fact, I think it's less, and it's perfectly acceptable!"

"Well, I suppose it might have something to do with the wearer. I've seen guys in them who should be arrested. I like it. It looks good on you, and you look good in it. In fact, I'm really getting turned on!"

"Stop! Stop right there—that's just what Lori said, and this thing is driving me crazy!"

"Why or how did Neil talk you into it?"

"Oh, it came with a price—an extra grand plus a voucher for a three-day weekend, including airfare—all from the club manager."

"Presidents' Day?" Margaret asked excitedly, jumping up and giving him a hug. "You mean you did that for me? That's so sweet."

Neither of them knew who realized it first or who was more surprised when Margaret jumped up to hug him and the front of her suit fell to her waist. At least it was tight enough that it didn't fall past her hips. Suddenly, they were both aware that they were holding each other, bare skin to bare skin.

Then she kissed him, and he returned the kiss. Margaret wasn't going to be the first to release the embrace, and it seemed that Rich was in no hurry either.

After a long minute, he asked, "With both of us standing here half-naked, do we risk getting arrested?"

"I don't care. I want to stay like this all afternoon," Margaret whispered, still surprised that he hadn't release his hold.

"Well, one of us needs to get back to work—and one of us needs to pull up the straps of her swimming suit." He reached for them and helped her slip her arms through. Then he picked up his towel and tied it around his waist.

"Behave yourself!" he said in a hoarse whisper, playfully pushing her back to her lounge chair. "And thank you for helping me prove my theory."

"What theory?" She looked at him suspiciously as she pulled him down beside her.

"Remember when I told you that I've always wanted to sneak up to a girl on the beach and dump cold water on her back to see if she jumps up so fast that I can see her breasts?"

"Oh yeah, that. What are you, back in the seventh grade?"

"Maybe eighth—but now I know that it's not only something cold—but the possibility of a trip. What makes you think it's for you? Maybe Stan has a free weekend coming up."

"After what just happened, just you try to bring someone else—especially after I've seen you in that thong. Oh, yes, this is going to be good. I'll get some copies from Neil. This should be worth the trip and maybe four or five foot massages a week!"

"Oh yeah—just you try to prove it's me," he retorted, putting on the fake glasses and nose.

"I don't think I'll have any trouble getting people to believe it's you! A poster-sized print just opposite the cash register so everyone will see it, and I can look at it all day. Just think!"

"Okay, uncle, uncle—you can come back down. In fact, I may give the voucher to Neil just to make sure I get all the proofs! I trust that Lori about as far as I can throw her!"

"How much longer?"

"I don't know. I think we're pretty close to wrapping up, at least for all the stuff out here. They're going to want me in a shirt and slacks a little bit later."

He started to get up and then sat beside Margaret again, leaned in, and kissed her cheek.

Margaret dozed off but woke when she realized that someone was standing nearby. It was Neil. "What's up?"

"I've got a proposition for you. Don't say no until you hear me out."

"Shoot."

"That's just what I want to do. I want to shoot you, the two of you—but to do some full shots, like regular people, sitting having dinner, sitting at the bar, listening to music, walking on the beach, lying by the pool. I want to do some really classy couple shots like you'd find in some of those bride's magazines … you know, two people on their honeymoon. We're down here, and Rich said he'd do it if you agreed to do it with him."

Margaret sat up. "Rich said he would let you shoot his face, let you shoot him as a real person? He actually said that?"

"He said that if you would do it—if you thought it was a good idea—he'd do it. What do you say? I'll send Lori into town with you and get some more clothes if you think you don't have the right things. She brought some of the long wigs—the good ones. I don't know why, but I'm glad she did. Rich said he didn't have anything except the light and dark khakis, shorts, and his shirts, so I told him we'd find him a jacket, and he got all excited. I've never ever seen him excited about anything, but when I told him I'd get him a sports coat—well that's when he said he'd do it."

"You want to see him excited? Invite him to dig a hole. Okay, I guess I'm game. But only if it's going to be nice stuff. Neil, I know you're not going to pull something funny, but I'll agree only if you promise it will only be top-drawer stuff, nothing silly."

"Scout's honor," Neil swore, showing the palm of his hand and crossing his heart. "I'll have Lori start making a list of the clothes she thinks we'll need. You let her know what you have."

An hour later, Margaret, Lori, and Rich were in a car, being driven to a small, upscale shopping center. Lori and Margaret started looking for the dress and skirt they thought would round out her wardrobe for the photo shoot. Rich went to the men's department, desperate to find a jacket that would fit him.

He found the jacket. It was a linen and silk blend, almost white, closer to the color of cream. It fit him across the shoulders and chest, but he thought the sleeves were a little long, which surprised him. He wore it to where the girls were finishing picking out Margaret's clothes.

"What do you think?"

"Turn around," Lori told him. She ran her palm across his shoulders. "Okay, turn around again." She tugged at the sleeves, flattened a lapel, and buttoned the top button. "The sleeves are a little long, but if we can't get them shortened by this afternoon, they'll have to do. This must have been made to fit a gorilla—sorry—I mean I guess it would be easier to shorten a sleeve and take it in a little than to have too many jackets that were too small for bigger guys."

Rich turned again. "You know, I've always wanted one of these—since I first saw *Casablanca* and my first Bond movie. A white dinner jacket, a beautiful woman, a martini, and champagne cocktails for everyone—now that's living!"

"Not much call for that sort of thing in Wyoming, was there?" asked Lori.

"Well, not for the jacket and martini—or the champagne cocktail, anyway!" added Margaret.

"Hey, wasn't *Dr. No* filmed here in Jamaica? Have you seen *Casablanca*? Ever notice how many drinks are ordered one after another, and no one drinks them? They just order more drinks!"

"What are you talking about? It's funny, Rich, somehow I would have imagined you were the kind of guy to have come up with lime green or yellow and brown windowpane checks or something with hideous stripes or embroidering."

"Oh, I've already got all of those. Hey! I went to Arizona State—not some clown college!"

"Okay, let's see if we can get it fixed yet this afternoon. Find yourself a couple of shirts, and let's get out of here," Lori ordered, already looking for the alterations department.

The store specialized in doing things quickly, catering to a cruise ship and weekend tourist crowd that required a quick turnaround. Lori paid for everything, and they headed back to the hotel. The jacket would be delivered before seven o'clock.

Margaret and Rich quickly changed into the clothes that Lori and Neil suggested. Shirt and slacks, and a skirt and blouse for Margaret. Neil wanted to get some shots on the beach as the sun set and then at the bar. It surprised Rich and Margaret that the sun set so early. They would have almost two more hours of daylight in New York. By six thirty, they were well into dusk.

After the jacket arrived, there was another change of shirts, and Margaret put on the newly purchased dress as the couple sat first in the lounge, then on the terrace, and then in the restaurant.

At around eight o'clock, they were finished with all that Neil wanted to take that day. Everyone decided that they would meet in the bar later in the evening. Rich couldn't remember how many times he'd changed clothes that afternoon.

Sam had suggested that he wear one of the swimming suits—the blue one—so he could change right out in the open, without having to return to his room each time they were ready for another shot. Again, Rich could not understand how wearing a skimpy bikini was acceptable in public while a pair of white cotton briefs was not.

"We should all go over to that place called Rick's Café," Lori suggested, looking over her piña colada and pointing toward the terrace. "It's one of those places where people jump off the cliff into the sea."

"Jump off a cliff—drunk or sober?" Sam asked.

"To be honest with you, Lori, in my younger and dumber days, I would have been the first one out there, fully dressed, swimming suit, it wouldn't have mattered. I'd have been there trying not to kill myself while doing something stupid like it was nobody's business," Rich said.

"How tall is this cliff?" Margaret asked. She was sitting between Neil and Lori and had to twist around to make eye contact with her. "On a bet, I once dove—jumped off the ten-meter platform in the pool at URI. Would it be higher than that?"

"You did something on a bet?" Sam asked. "Suddenly I'm seeing you in a whole different light."

"I do lots of things," Margaret shot back, giving him a playful kick under the table. "And that different light you're seeing is coming from too many of those rum punches."

"A few more of these, and maybe I *will* jump off that cliff."

"You'd have to be crazy," said Neil, sounding like the only adult in a group of seven-year-olds. "Besides, there will be no cliff diving tonight. We have too much work to do tomorrow, and I don't want to waste the money that I spent on that new jacket if Rich were to go and kill himself jumping off a cliff. It's been altered, so the store won't take it back, and I doubt there's another human being on the island right now that it would fit or who would look as good in it."

Rich blushed. "Thanks, Neil."

"Hey, I'm not thinking about you. I'm thinking about that jacket. You wanna jump off a cliff, do it on your own time—but this trip, this entire trip, you all belong to me."

Everyone laughed.

"You know, I could get very used to this," Neil confessed as he leaned back in his chair. He and Rich were drinking straight rum while the others had tropical drinks in front of them. "Except for the steel drums," he added.

"What do you mean?" Lori asked. "They make the scene. You can't come to Jamaica or anywhere in the Caribbean and not have music!"

"No—I love the sound of steel drums, and I'm warming to reggae—at least some of it."

"But it's too loud, right? Sam asked.

"Exactly—that's it," Neil answered, suddenly sitting upright and snapping his fingers. "I've been sitting here all evening trying to figure out what was wrong. They're too loud. I'd like them a whole lot better if they were out on the terrace somewhere—off over there so that the music sort of floated over instead of hitting you between the eyes."

"You know, we could always go and sit on the terrace on the other side of the pool," Margaret suggested.

"No—too far from the bar!" Sam pointed out as he held up his glass for the waiter to see.

"For me, steel drums are like the sound of a bagpipe. I love it, but it's something that should be heard from a distance—across the glen—across the water and trees—like I said, sort of floating on the air instead of banging you in the head."

"Gee, Neil, I never knew you were so poetic," Lori teased as the waiter approached with a tray full of refills.

"*Presidents' Day weekend*," Margaret mouthed to Rich, sitting across from her as she bounced her eyebrows and rubbed her bare foot against his calf.

13

"Do you want to go over to Grand Central?" Rich asked as he pulled a couple of beers and seltzers out of the refrigerator.

"No, you go ahead," Margaret answered. "I'm going to pack. The car is coming early in the morning. The train's at seven. I'll just finish this and maybe catch up with you later. Hey, do you want to come to Baltimore with me?"

She always asked him to come with her when she went on an out-of-town photo shoot. He almost always declined the invitation. "I don't want to be in the way," he would always tell her.

"You know you won't be in the way. You could go to the Inner Harbor and eat crab cakes, maybe take in a ball game—I've always wanted to see Camden Yards—or you could just crash in the hotel," she said.

"I'll feel like a kept boy, and people would talk," he joked.

"What's wrong with being a kept boy? If someone offered me a chance to get away, all expenses paid, I'd just ask when, where, and for how long?"

"So would I, but it seems different when I'd just be tagging along."

"You wouldn't be just—well, you would be, I guess, but that wouldn't matter to Neil or the crew. All they'd be out is a couple of meals—and I'd pay for those if it would make it any easier on you."

"See, why would you think you would have to pay for my meals? It's not the money. And I don't mind you coming with me, so it's not the sharing a room either—well—just forget about it because I'm not going. Maybe I'll call Mike and take the train out to Montauk or someplace."

"You'd go out there without me?"

"What?"

They both loved Montauk, and they always went together, whether to spend a day or a weekend. There was something about the rocky beaches and the quiet during the off season. Margaret loved sitting in front of the fire with a class of cognac after dinner. Rich loved the pounding surf and the idea that there was nothing but water between him and England or Spain or whatever was out there.

"You still love her, don't you?"

He looked at her like she had just said something very terribly wrong.

"What do you mean?" he asked, with surprise and hurt in his voice.

"Hey, I don't mean anything by it … but, you still love Sandy."

He put the two cans of beer that he was holding back into the refrigerator and walked out the door.

After a few minutes, probably the time it took Rich to walk down to the corner and back, she heard him unlock the door. She thought he would go straight to his bedroom, but he didn't. She heard him walk to the kitchen and retrieve a can of beer and a bottle of seltzer and pour them into glasses. Margaret walked out of her room and saw him sitting on the sofa, staring into space. She walked over, and he handed her one of the glasses as she sat next to him.

"Give me a different word."

"What?"

"You said that I still loved Sandy. Give me a different word—I'm not sure that love is the right one."

Margaret thought for a couple of minutes. "Carrying a torch … pining … longing? I don't know," she admitted.

"Longing? I guess I'm still thinking of her. I can't help it." He looked at the wedding ring that he still wore.

"Hey, you do still love her. There's nothing wrong with that. But you're going to have to get on with your life. She left you, remember?"

Rich started to get up but then sat back down, this time a little closer to Margaret.

"I know that. I knew it was over a long time ago, but I just can't let her go—not like this. If she had died, if she was remarried and happy—I don't even know where she is. Do you know that sometimes when we're out walking or in Grand Central, I think I see her? I imagine that someday she'll walk in the door and order a burger—that she'll say she's sorry." He turned toward Margaret. "And what scares me the most—scares me to death—is that I won't know how to react—how I should—she'll say that she's sorry, and I won't know what to say."

Margaret put her head on his shoulder.

"You'll know what to say, but," she paused, carefully weighing her words, "it's been a long time, and I doubt she'll ever come …" Margaret stopped; she'd said too much.

"You're right, I know you're right. I don't know how long it will take, but I'll get over her someday, and you'll be the first to know."

He touched her hand, drank his beer, and left, locking the door behind him as he always did, so that he wouldn't forget his keys. Margaret finished packing and wished he would change his mind.

After she dropped her bag near the door, she went to the refrigerator and put two cans of beer and a bottle of seltzer along with some ice in the little cooler that they carried to Grand Central and walked over to try to find Rich.

He was sitting on the steps as he usually did, listening to his favorite pair of musicians who played in the station on most Friday evenings. It was a young couple; he played the guitar, and she played the violin, and oh, could they make them sing! He took her hand as she sat next to him.

"Take as long as you need. I'm willing to—going to wait for you. You can't push me away, and I won't let you. You're mine, and until you're ready, I'll be here waiting for you."

"M, do you think it's too late to call Neil and tell him I'm coming to Baltimore?"

14

A week before Thanksgiving, Rich surprised Margaret by suggesting that they rent a car and drive to Kentucky. She knew he had plans to fly home at Christmas while she joined her family at her sister's home in Atlanta.

"I'll take off work Thursday and Friday, and we could leave on Wednesday, drive all night, and get there by dinnertime. I just want to get out of town for a couple of days. You do have Thanksgiving dinner at your house, don't you?"

At first she was puzzled. Of course they had planned to be closed on Thursday and Friday, even possibly closing a little early on Wednesday if things got slow, which they probably would. She didn't understand what Rich was talking about. Then she realized that the European markets would not be closed and that he would have been expected to be in the office over the American holiday.

"Why, yes," she answered, in her best southern drawl, "and all the young men line up and ask the ladies to eat barbecue with them, and we all make such a fuss while we're supposed to be upstairs resting before the big dance, while all the men stand around the parlor talking secession and smoking cigars."

"That's what I thought. Well, I really have my heart set on a turkey dinner with lots of bourbon before, during, and after. I won't have to get dressed up or anything, will I?"

"No, dressed up on Thanksgiving is whatever you happen to be wearing. I think the last time I was home, my sister's husband showed up in hunting clothes. It sounds like fun. I hope the weather is okay. I'd hate to get stuck in the mountains someplace." She'd lost the drawl.

"I'll call mother and tell her to get a bigger turkey and set two extra places at the table." The drawl was back. "She'll be so happy that I'm finally bringing a man home—even if it is only you—it will be such a spectacle! I'm sure that they will all be surprised that you'll want to use the guestroom, and then will actually use it!"

"Will that be a problem? I could always sleep in the servants' quarters or go to a motel." He'd met her parents but none of the other members of her family.

"We don't have servants or quarters, and no, you will not get a motel room—that would just kill my already ruined reputation. I know that Mother will enjoy the fuss, but Daddy will be relieved. I'm sure he's put his shotgun away for the season—unless there's a feud going on somewhere!"

Rich laughed until the tears ran down his cheeks.

Wednesday afternoon finally rolled around. It had been a really slow day with so many people taking off early and getting a head start on the holiday.

The gray sky promised a cold rain as Rich pulled the rented car up to the front of the building and honked the horn. Margaret thought about throwing her small duffel bag out the window like they were making some sort of escape but though better of it. He had left his bag just inside the door before he went to the rental agency and had already put it in the trunk by the time Margaret came through the door, locking it behind her. Rich left the car running as he took her bags, tossed them in the trunk with his, and held the door for her after she carefully laid her coat on the backseat, on top of the coat that he'd simply thrown in.

"Have I told you that I love this coat and I love you?"

"Once or twice—the coat I mean. One way or another, you tell me you love me every day," He leaned inside the car and gave her a peck on the cheek.

"What kind of car is this? I didn't really pay attention, but it's outrageously extravagant!" Margaret commented once Rich had gotten behind the wheel.

"Some kind of Oldsmobile; there's a number that's part of the name, but I don't remember it. It's a lot bigger than we need, but I thought it'd be a little more comfortable than a regular sedan."

"An Oldsmobile!" Margaret said. "Won't Daddy be impressed?" She reached out to adjust the heat. "I'm surprised you didn't get some sort of truck!" Seeing the CD player, she added, "If I'd thought about it, I would have brought some discs. Or were you planning to sing?"

Rich handed her a CD case with a mixed collection of discs.

"Well then, let's hit the road," she said as she adjusted the electric seat and reclined. "Did you remember to bring your golf clubs—tennis racquet? Let's see, what else do we southerners do for recreation?"

"Hunt foxes?"

"That's it. Did you bring a saddle?"

"Saddle? I didn't think of that. Should I go back and pick it up or do you think I can borrow one?" He didn't wait for an answer before he put the car in gear and pulled into traffic.

"You don't really have a saddle here in New York, do you?"

"Do you think that just because I ride horses, I'd carry a saddle around? Is that what you think of cowboys? Do you think I'd have chaps and a gun and a ten-gallon hat? You saw me move in. Did you see any of that?"

Margaret smiled. "Well, don't you have everything you just mentioned?"

"Well, sure, and now that you mention it, I could probably wear them in New York, and no one would notice."

"Except for the saddle."

"Except for the saddle," he admitted as they crossed Times Square. "Now that I think about it, I don't have a cowboy hat here either," he said. They headed for the West Side Highway and the George Washington Bridge, which would take them across the Hudson River, into New Jersey, and onto Interstate 80, toward Pennsylvania.

Traffic was heavy as they drove through the outer townships but then began to lighten as they got farther from the city. It was already dark, and the wind began to pick up, invisible through the leafless trees. Margaret turned on the little map light and studied the road atlas that Rich had purchased.

"Do you know where you're going or are you planning to drive west until you see a sign for Cincinnati?" Margaret asked as she inserted another CD, placing Dire Straits back in the carrier.

"Well, that was my plan, but I guess you're going to change it."

"I've never driven this way before. I've always gone on a weekend and headed down past Philadelphia and then through Maryland and on to West Virginia."

"We may take that way coming back on Saturday, but I didn't want to be on the Jersey Turnpike with all that traffic. I'm sure it would be bumper-to-bumper, and I didn't even want to think about what the tunnels would be like."

They headed west and then south, changing to the Pennsylvania Turnpike outside of Harrisburg. It started to rain.

"This may have been a mistake. I hope we make it through the mountains before things get icy. I think it's pretty near freezing. How many people does your mother expect?"

Margaret again turned on her best southern drawl. "Well, there will be Mother and Daddy, Daddy's brother, Philip, and his wife, Angela, my grandparents—that makes six. The two of us, that makes eight, and my sister Virginia, her husband, Reginald Herbert Andrew Jackson Greenside, the Fourth, heir to Greenside Farms of Paris, Kentucky, and their two children."

Rich stole a glance out of the corner of his eye. "You're kidding, right?"

"Oh, no, there will be twelve for dinner."

"I mean, Reginald what's-his-name the Fourth?"

"No, that's his name. My sister is Virginia Stephanie Belinda Waller-Greenside, Mrs. Reginald Herbert Andrew Jackson Greenside, the Fourth, heir to the Greenside Farms of Paris, Kentucky—thank you very much."

"And what are or is the Greenside Farms? I've known you for how long, and this is the first time I'm hearing about your sister and her husband's farm?"

"Don't tell me you've never heard of the famous Greenside Farms of Paris, Kentucky? Why it is one of the richest, most successful, and famous of the old family Kentucky horse farms. They have had five Derby winners and sired four others, including a Triple Crown Winner. To hear Reginald's mother talk, you'd think that she rode and won the Derby twice herself!"

"Wow, sounds like your sister really caught a big one."

"Oh, Ginny's the pretty one of the family. She could have had anyone she wanted. Reginald is the lucky one. The Greensides are traditionally not much to look at. After awhile, they started looking a lot like their horses."

Rich was laughing as Tracy Chapman played on the stereo.

"You'll see tomorrow. Just be sure you don't stand too close to Reggie while you're holding an apple. He may snatch it right out of your hand with those big horse teeth of his. I can't believe that with all that money, his parents didn't get that boy to an orthodontist! Oh, and don't call him Reginald, at least not in his presence. I think he got beat up a lot as a child because of that name. Granddaddy says that he hopes the two of them have enough sense not to name their daughter Winifred; a great-granddaughter called Whinny would surely be the ruin of the family. The first two are boys, but who knows about the next."

"Well, I haven't met all of your family, but I'll bet that you're the pretty one, and I hope they're not too disappointed in you bringing only me." He put his hand on hers.

"Are you kidding?" Margaret turned so she could face him, just as the chorus of "Fast Car" continued, *"And your arm felt nice wrapped 'round my shoulder. And I had a feeling that I belonged ..."*

She pushed the armrest into the seat back, released the seatbelt and shoulder strap, moved closer, took his hand, and put it over her shoulder as she leaned against him. She was surprised that he didn't take his arm away as she snuggled close and buckled the middle belt around her waist.

"That's nice, but the airbag won't do you a lot of good way over here."

"I'm not worried. Besides, I'll take my chances for the chance to sit here like this. Now, where was I? Oh yes—and by the way, never disturb a girl when she's giving her opinion, advice, or being catty! Have I told you that I love to see you in that shirt? It really looks good on you—not as good as a plain white T-shirt with those jeans but almost."

"You gave me this shirt!"

"I know. Have I told you how much I love it—and how much I love you?" she asked.

"Where have I heard that question before? The shirt—every time I wear it—and me—at least once a day."

"But you'll have to do better than that. A girl likes to be reminded of these things," she continued. "They are so excited about meeting you, they just can't wait. After all, you are an athlete. Granddaddy loves athletes. And a foreign investment analyst. Well, that will just be a wonderful combination in everyone's book, although I'm not sure they all know what a foreign investment analyst really is or does, but that won't matter. It sounds impressive.

"I think the closest Reginald Herbert, the Fourth, came to being an athlete was playing in the University of Louisville pep band at basketball games—the saxophone, I believe. Luckily it's one of those instruments that no one drags out to play for you. That's another strike against him of course. It is still a mystery to some members of the family how and why Judge Waller ever allowed his eldest daughter to date, much less marry, a Louisville Cardinal, even if he was a Greenside of Paris, Kentucky. And Lawyer, well, Lawyer was just too busy studying to care about athletes except when he was placing bets on their games."

"The lawyer? Who's that?"

"Not the lawyer but Lawyer. That's his name. Lawyer Stephen Davis Lee, MD, husband of my other sister, Patricia: Patricia Viola Elizabeth Waller-Lee of Atlanta, Georgia."

"That's his name, that's really his name? Sorry I asked! Does he go by 'Larry'?"

"No, it's Lawyer. Oh and don't you worry. My grandparents will just love you to pieces. You already know my parents do. That is, as long as you don't bring up the War of Northern Aggression, basketball at the Universities of Louisville, Xavier, or Cincinnati, or become a vegetarian. You don't have any relatives who fought for the North, do you? You're middle name isn't Lincoln or Abraham or Ulysses, Sheridan, Mead, or Yankee, is it? Bad enough we live in New York with those Yankees always winning the World Series! Although, I love rubbing it into the Lees of Atlanta."

"I'm a Mets and Cardinals fan, and I believe that Pete Rose should be in the Hall of Fame. Does that help my cause?"

"That will help a little, but don't bring it up if no one asks."

She started to fumble with the heat, trying to get more warm air to her feet. He moved his right arm and adjusted the controls. "How's that?"

"Better. Just make it warmer; it doesn't have to blow so hard. You'll want to keep a little blowing on the windshield, won't you?"

He put his arm back across her shoulder. "I put a blanket on the backseat. You want it?"

"No, I'm okay." She snuggled a little closer to him and went to sleep.

The album ended. Rich lowered the volume and switched from the CD player to the radio, tuned into a sports talk station, and adjusted the heat; it was getting too warm. He reached into the backseat for the blanket and unfolded it over Margaret, best he could with one hand. When he'd finished, he put his arm back over her shoulder, the words of the song echoing in his head, "... *leave tonight or live and die this way. And I had a feeling I belonged. And I had a feeling that I could be someone, be someone ...*"

He stopped for gas just outside Washington, Pennsylvania. After filling the tank, Rich pulled the car to the front of the station. It was cold, but the rain had stopped long ago.

"What time is it and where are we?"

"A little before three, and we're just on the other side of Washington, almost to West Virginia. We left the turnpike a little while ago. Now we're on the interstate, right about here." He pointed to the map. "I'm gonna get something to drink. You want anything?"

"Yes, no—yes, get me something warm. If they have hot chocolate, that would be great."

"Okay, I'll be right back." He left the car running. "Lock the doors."

He returned a few minutes later with a cup of cocoa, a bottle of cola, a small package of beef jerky, and four chocolate bars. "Midnight snacks of champions! I think there's a cup holder here somewhere."

"I could never understand how people eat this stuff," Margaret said as she opened the jerky, using her teeth to tear the top of the package.

"That's just the point. You don't eat it; you chew it. It gives your mouth something to do besides talk. You know us cowboys—men of few words."

"I thought you were supposed to sing to the cows to keep them calm or something like that. That's what they always did in the movies."

"That's what Roy Rogers might have done. Where I come from, that sort of thing would get you an ass whooping. Have a piece, but I don't know how it will go with that cocoa."

They made better time than they thought they would and arrived in Cincinnati at seven o'clock on Thanksgiving morning. They crossed the Ohio River and made their way to Kenton Hills.

"How does that go? 'Last night I returned to Manderley.' How many families live here?" Rich asked as they turned onto the driveway.

"Oh, stop it, it's not that big."

Margaret's mother, Ellen, was already awake, having just put the turkey in the oven a few minutes earlier. She showed Rich to the guestroom and invited him to have a nap before the rest of the house became busy. He was happy to accept the invitation after driving through the night.

Margaret, having slept a good part of the way, was ready to help with preparing dinner. Rich slept for almost three hours and then showered, shaved, and came to the kitchen wearing a dark blue oxford shirt and dark chinos. He volunteered to help, and they put him right to work peeling potatoes.

Last year, when he first met her, Rich could see that Margaret got her good looks from her mother. She was a beautiful woman. And when he first met her father, it was easy to see where Margaret got her height. Charles Waller stood six feet five and had the hands of someone who had handled many basketballs over the years. Unfortunately, he also had the knees of someone who had pounded up and down a floor in his younger and middle years. He'd had both replaced.

Everyone else soon arrived, and the women all gathered in the kitchen, taking on the various tasks of preparing the dinner.

"Okay," Charles advised, "you've got the potatoes peeled; now it's time for the men to clear out and leave the women to their gossip.

They can call you when they're ready to mash. Your ears are going to be burning pretty soon."

He led Rich to the dining room where his brother, father, son-in-law, and two grandsons were busy setting the table. Without thinking, Rich picked up a stack of folded linen napkins and quickly refolded them into a fleur-de-lis and placed them on the dinner plates. Everyone had stopped what they were doing and stood and watched as he worked his way around the table.

"What?" he asked as he realized that he was suddenly the center of attention, finishing the last napkin.

"Well, it's eleven o'clock. I'm sure the drinking light is lit someplace. It doesn't seem too early to have a cocktail!" Uncle Phil said, breaking the silence. The men all agreed and moved from the dining room to the den where the bar and the television were waiting. The grandsons headed to the basement and their video games.

Awhile later, Margaret appeared and asked Rich to come into the kitchen.

"It's time to take the turkey out of the oven." She smiled as she led him through the dining room. "Mother asked me to ask you if you would give us a hand."

Rich didn't say anything but felt five pairs of eyes boring down on him as he was handed the oven mitts, opened the oven, and lifted the turkey onto the top of the stove.

"Anything else?" he asked as he turned to see everyone watching him.

"Well, yes, the potatoes need to be mashed, but they can wait a few more minutes," Margaret's mother told him.

"I was being checked out, wasn't I?" Rich asked as she walked him back to the den.

"Yeah, you were."

"How'd I do?"

"I don't know yet. Let me get back in there and find out."

Dinner was an informal banquet. Rich wasn't sure whether it was always like this on the holidays or whether Margaret's mother went out of her way for him. He got his wish, and there was plenty of bourbon before, during, and after dinner. Margaret's father, Charles, was an authority on good Kentucky bourbon and had several special bottles that he invited Rich and the other members of the family to sample.

Charles's father, who had also been a judge, now long retired, told them the story of the number of stills that abounded throughout northern Kentucky during Prohibition and the number that were still operating today. Margaret goaded Rich into telling the funny story that he'd once told her, about a disastrous Thanksgiving that he'd had in Wyoming.

After dinner, there were football games to be watched while Margaret continued to catch up with the news and gossip with her mother, grandmother, aunt, and older sister.

Later in the afternoon, Margaret volunteered to drive her grandparents back to their home. The Greensides left at eight, and Uncle Phil and Aunt Angela made their farewells soon after, inviting them all to join them for dinner on Friday night.

The house was quiet, and the four of them sat in the light of the fireplace. They could see the lights of Cincinnati across the Ohio River. There was more bourbon for a nightcap before Ellen excused herself and retired for the night. Charles followed her a few minutes later.

"You've got to be tired," Margaret whispered as she closed the doors on the fireplace, letting the flames die down. She sat next to him on the sofa.

"I am, but not exhausted. I think it's mainly from all that turkey. This was a great day. I'm glad we came—and you know what?" He put his arm around her and pulled her close. "I've only met one of your sisters, but I do believe that you got the looks in the family."

They sat in silence a few minutes more, watching the dying fire and the city lights across the way.

"Was the choice of that shirt an accident or on purpose?"

"What do you mean?" he asked, raising his arm and looking at the sleeve.

"Dark blue—University of Kentucky blue. Don't think that was overlooked by Daddy!"

"I certainly didn't mean anything by it. I've always thought it was French blue—I had no idea it was also Kentucky blue. I guess that's how I'll refer to this color from now on."

"You will if you know what's good for you—from now on!"

They all slept late on Friday. Anything after two in the morning was late for Rich, but after driving all night and eating that huge dinner, he was able to sleep even after the house began to stir.

"What are your plans for today?" Margaret's mother asked as Rich poured himself a cup of coffee.

"No plans," he answered, lowering himself onto one of the chairs at the kitchen table.

"Well, Margaret wants to go shopping—I don't know why. She lives in New York. Tell me there's anything we have here that she couldn't find there?"

"Who knows? Maybe something local. You know what I'd really like to do, and I know this is going to sound dumb, but I'd love to go to the zoo and see those tigers."

"The tigers, you mean the white Bengals? That's not so silly; I think it's a great idea. If you want to go, I'm sure Charlie will go with you. I know he won't go shopping with us. And it would give you two a chance to get to know each other a little better."

"Well, if you don't mind me saying, I don't know why anyone would want to go shopping on today of all days. Won't the stores be packed?"

"But that's the best time. Here, and I suppose it's like that all over, shopping is a social thing. It's not so much about buying something—it's shopping! Watching people—being part of the crowd is part of the whole experience and as important as the shopping itself. We'll get dressed up to go to the mall down in Florence—because that's what's expected."

"Now you're beginning to sound like Margaret. She puts on this southern belle act like she's in *Gone with the Wind* or something."

"Honey," Ellen explained with a smile as warm and soft as anything he'd seen, letting her drawl hang in the air as she sat next to him, "do not ever underestimate the power of a belle's charm. When she wants to turn it on, well watch out, and when she wants to turn it off—well you'd just better hope that you're not around when she does. And never call it an act. That's breeding. It can never be learned; it can only be refined." Ellen's smile warmed even more, and she looked so much more like Margaret's sister than her mother.

"Margaret loves you very much. I hope you don't mind me saying that."

"Mrs. Waller—"

"Ellen, please."

"Ellen, there's something I have to tell you, something you have to know."

"Richard," she put her hand on his, "we know all about you. Margaret told us a long time ago—long before you moved in with her. We know you're not living together but only sharing an apartment. We had a long talk yesterday while you were resting, before the others arrived. She loves you, and we love you, and we all want to help you through this so the two of you can be together and be happy. Our Margaret invited you to move in with her because she wanted to be close to you and wanted you close to her.

"She told us all about it, and we're very happy for her after everything that happened before." She leaned a little closer, looking him in the eyes. "And don't try to make her let you go. Her mind is made up. You're the one—and, well, when one of my girls, especially Margaret, sets her heart on something or someone, there's no getting away."

Rich didn't know what to say. He only remembered the number of times that he had been a jerk and pushed Margaret away. Fortunately, Margaret came into the kitchen, soon followed by her father.

The zoo wasn't crowded, and Rich was happy that Charles was interested in not much more than light conversation—the weather, football, the first weeks of the college basketball season. Rich asked about his being a judge—was it an elected or appointed position—where the courthouse was located—just light banter. Somewhere along the way, Rich realized that Charles didn't ask personal questions about him because he already knew a lot. Margaret had apparently kept her parents well informed just as she had done with Roxanne and Stan.

Rich and Margaret started out for the return trip to New York early on Saturday morning. The day was cold, gray, and damp, and there was the threat of rain in Kentucky and snow and ice across the Blue Ridge. Rich wanted to get an early start and get back to New York before they got caught in bad weather, so he decided to take the southern route across West Virginia and Maryland before heading north through Pennsylvania, still wanting to avoid I-95 and the Jersey Turnpike.

Margaret did most of the talking on the way home, filling Rich in on all the family news and gossip that she had heard from her sister and grandmother. Rich just listened. All of it mattered because he had never met any of those people, and he enjoyed hearing how excited Margaret got while talking about this or that cousin.

After a couple of hours, Margaret had talked herself out and fell asleep, nestled against him. He played with the radio and found a football game that kept him entertained for another hour.

Somewhere around Allentown, with the chorus of "Fast Car" still playing in his head from two days ago—*"You gotta make a decision. Leave tonight or live and die this way"*—he knew that he had to make a change. Rich couldn't deny what he was feeling, especially after hearing what Ellen had told him the day before.

15

Christmas season in New York officially began at Thanksgiving, although many of the stores had been decorated since before Halloween. There was something really special about being in the city during the weeks leading up to Christmas.

The tree in Rockefeller Center was lit in early December, and the entire city appeared trimmed in lights. The giant menorah on Fifty-Ninth was lit for Hanukah, and the huge UNICEF snowflake was suspended above the intersection of Fifty-Seventh and Fifth.

People gathered in front of store windows to see the different displays. As the holidays drew nearer, the city became that much more crowded.

On the Monday after Thanksgiving, they got back to their routine. Rich went to the office, after being off for four days, and they served hundreds of hamburgers and hot dogs at lunchtime, just like usual.

As Christmas approached, there were a number of office parties, and business began to drop off, little by little, as people began to escape the city for the holidays. It made it easy for them to keep to their plans of closing a few days before Christmas Eve and get away themselves. Margaret was going to fly to Atlanta to spend Christmas with her family gathering at her sister's home. She was anxious to hear the "buzz" over Rich and get the reaction of her sisters. She'd said there would be a lot of gossip while the boys were out playing golf and placing bets on football games.

Margaret's Christmas in Atlanta felt like it was scripted. There were visits to Stone Mountain and a walk through Centennial Olympic Park to see the lights and watch the ice skaters.

Margaret wasn't familiar with Atlanta, having visited her sister and her family only twice since they had relocated to Georgia. She was happy that her sister had almost every part of the days planned so that she could simply be along for the ride. On the twenty-fourth, everything seemed rushed. As strange as it seemed, however, having Christmas Eve dinner in a casual restaurant turned out to be a relaxing time.

Christmas Day, in the kitchen, Margaret's sister Patricia tried to pass off the dinner rolls as her own fresh baked. She might have gotten away with it if, when they were all seated for dinner, Dr. Lee—Lawyer—hadn't commented on how many stores he had visited before he found the right ones—and how he would have preferred biscuits. Patty would have a difficult time living that down.

There was baked ham, candied sweet potatoes, along with the traditional green bean casserole and pecan pie. There was even a molded green gelatin salad that, for some reason, Margaret could not help but imagine was straight out of a 1960s television show.

Rich headed home to Wyoming where he looked forward to the mountains, snow, being on a horse, a fireplace, and the possibility of an elk hunt. He had not seen his sister and her family for a couple of years and couldn't wait to be with his family at the Christmas dinner his mom would prepare. Tradition in their family called for pizza on Christmas Eve and roasted wild geese for Christmas dinner. And of course, there was the trip to Cheyenne and Home Depot with his dad and brother.

Christmas dinner was all that he'd hoped it would be; his sister and her husband and kids were there, his parents and his brother with his new girlfriend, along with the three winter ranch hands. As Rich looked around, he could feel that all of them—his parents, his sister and brother-in-law, his brother and his girl—were so much in love. Of course, that was what Christmas was all about—getting together with family. All of it fueled what he was feeling inside—the flame that had been kindled that morning in November.

Everyone had questions about New York. His parents, of course, asked about Margaret and his trip to Kentucky at Thanksgiving. He filled them all in regarding Thanksgiving, the Firehouse, and his trip to Jamaica. He also told them about the weekend with Roxanne and Stan and how he and Margaret were getting along, growing closer. It was good to be home. The snow was deep, it was bitterly cold, and he was happy to be out doing chores, throwing hay to the cattle and horses.

It had been a very good month since Thanksgiving. Business was good, but he had a funny feeling in the pit of his stomach. Everything had changed, and Rich looked forward to the chance to get back to New York and do something about it.

Rich returned to the city on the twenty-eighth, and Margaret late on the twenty-ninth, having learned long ago that it was easier to get a flight back into New York before all the last-minute returnees. The weather was sometimes also a factor since they wanted to open up again on January 2, after the holidays were officially over in the city.

The weather was cold but clear. Margaret's Delta flight came up the coast, past the lower end of Manhattan, and up along the Hudson River before banking over Long Island Sound into La Guardia. It was depressing to see the skyline without the Twin Towers that had been such an important landmark for more than thirty years. The huge void that was once the World Trade Center provided an eerie reminder of what had happened. Margaret thought back to the first time that she flew over Manhattan after 9/11. Then there was still smoke rising out of the crater, and crews worked at cutting through and removing the twisted metal. That first time, she thought it must have been what it looked like in hell. At least now, in the winter twilight, it simply looked like a construction site.

There had been no new snow since before Christmas, and the streets and sidewalks were clear, ready for the celebration of New Year's Eve in Times Square—probably one of the greatest traditions in New York City.

Rick planned to go the gym late in the afternoon on the thirty-first. It would close at six, and he wanted to get in a good workout since he planned to do nothing but sit and watch football games all day on the first. Margaret decided to take a swim and said that she would join him at the gym, but she also wanted to walk through Times Square, take one last look at the tree in Rockefeller Center, and watch the skaters.

They walked holding hands, and he offered his arm each time they crossed a street. He was wearing his heavy, hooded pullover sweatshirt, a knit cap, and a dark cotton jacket. She loved seeing him with that hood pulled up, although she could not understand how he could be walking around in the cold wearing only his sweatpants. She was wearing her old quilted coat and the new cap that her grandmother had knitted for her. The weather was bitter cold, but there was festivity in the air.

As usual, Times Square was already filling with people. The sidewalks were crowded, and the only place left to walk was in the street, once it had been closed to traffic. After that, they headed for the gym—with the plan to stop for carryout Chinese on the way home and spend a quiet evening together.

"Those people are going to freeze tonight," Margaret said as she huddled closer to Rich as they walked from the gym to the restaurant.

"You're going to freeze walking around in wet hair," Rich answered.

"Oh, it's almost dry—and this hat is plenty warm."

When they got home, Rick put their workout clothes and towels in the washer. Earlier, he had put three bottles of Prosecco on the roof, as a surprise for later. He brought them into the kitchen, placed two in the refrigerator, and the third in a saucepan that would serve as an ice bucket. He filled the pan with ice and popped the cork. Margaret set the coffee table with plates, glasses, and their take-out food. It would be a feast.

By eleven o'clock, thanks to the long day and two bottles of wine, they were both asleep on the sofa. Margaret woke just before midnight and woke Rich. They watched the ball drop in Times Square, gave each other a Happy New Year kiss, and went to their rooms.

16

On the evening of January 2, after work and when Rich had returned from the gym, he found Margaret lying on the sofa, wrapped in her comforter, reading. He opened the third bottle of Prosecco, filled two glasses, handed one to her, and sat as he lifted and then laid her legs across his lap as he usually did. Tonight her feet were tightly wrapped in the quilt. Anita Baker was playing on the stereo. They sat in silence for about five minutes. He took a drink, almost draining his glass.

"I called a lawyer today," he said, turning toward her.

"What?" Margaret asked—the sip of wine that she'd just taken almost coming out of her nose.

"I called a lawyer today. Glenn—he comes in here a couple times a week. His office is over on Third Avenue. I meet with him on Wednesday afternoon. I decided to do it while I was home."

Margaret swung her legs off his lap and sat upright.

"Wait a minute. You decided *what* while you were home?"

"I decided it was time to make a change. Just like you said, I have to get on with my life, and I'm tired of pushing you away. I'm tired of making you say you're sorry for trying to help me. It's time."

"I don't understand! Just like that? What made you make up your mind?"

"It's not just like that. It's something I've been thinking about for a month. It's something I should have done a long time ago. You've been right all along."

They were both startled when the phone rang. Margaret started to reach for it, but he pulled her back down to the sofa.

"I'll get it," he said as he stood, turning toward the ringing. "Is your shoot in Boston this weekend?"

"No, it's next week," she answered as he picked up the phone. "Do you want to come along?" He frowned and shook his head.

"Oh, hi, Lauren!" he said.

"Richard?" Sandy's mother asked from Tucson. "Just a minute. Bill wants to get on the other line."

Sandy's father picked up the extension and said, "Richard … son, we got a call from a lawyer a little while ago."

Rich felt like someone had hit him in the stomach. His knees went weak, and he sat down heavily.

"Richard—Sandy's dead. She died just before Christmas—Christmas two years ago. Two years ago!" Bill said.

Rich slumped in the chair and turned toward Margaret, signaling her to pick up the phone on the desk.

"Richard, are you there, dear?" Sandy's mother asked. She was crying.

"How? What happened?" Rich asked.

"We don't know all the details yet. She made arrangements for this lawyer fellow to call us after two years—I don't know why she wanted him to wait. I guess she didn't want us to make a fuss, but she'd been sick for a long time—a long time," Bill answered.

"Her body was cremated," Lauren said, choking on the words. "They've made arrangements for her ashes, her remains to be sent home." There was a long pause. "Home here to Tucson."

"Richard, that's all we know right now," Bill said. "But there is something else. Sandy died of AIDS—or something brought on by the AIDS." There was a longer pause. "Did you hear me, son? Sandy had AIDS."

Lauren was sobbing. Rich and Margaret exchanged shocked looks, and Margaret started to cry, her hand covering her mouth.

"Margaret, is that you on the other line?" Bill asked. "Are you there?"

They had met only once, when Bill and Lauren came to New York for a visit. They had spent a weekend, staying in the extra bedroom, and the four of them had seen a Broadway musical and had dinner together.

"She's here, Bill," Rich assured him, feeling sick and confused. Margaret hung up the phone and pulled a chair over to where Rich was sitting, putting her ear up to the receiver that he held.

"Listen, son, we're going to call this lawyer tomorrow. You don't need to worry about that, but … he said we should call you right away and tell you to get tested—you and Margaret."

"He waited two years to tell me to get tested, and now he tells us it's urgent? He didn't think it should have been done right away—two years ago?" Rich asked, a wave of frustration and anger overcoming him.

"I asked the same question. He couldn't even if he wanted to—even in the interest of public health—that's what he told me anyway," Bill answered. "If you ask me, client privilege be damned, at least in a case like this."

"He may have thought that, after so long a time, you may not have had it," Lauren added. "That's the only thing that makes sense."

Margaret took the phone from Rich's hand as he slumped farther into the chair, the color draining from his body.

"Bill, Lauren, I'm so terribly sorry—I don't know what to say," Margaret said through her tears.

"We know, dear," Lauren answered. "We're just glad that you're there, that Richard isn't alone to hear this. Don't you worry about us; we've been waiting for something like this for a long time. I guess even if you expect bad news, you're never ready for it when it comes."

"Now, you two go and get yourselves checked," Bill said, "Do it right away. Do it tomorrow. The fellow told us that you and Sandy … that you might have been infected years ago—and now you …" Bill's voice faltered.

"Okay, we will, and don't worry about Rich. I'll take care of him tonight. We'll get through this," Margaret reassured them.

"Good-bye, Margaret. We're glad you're there to take care of him. We'll call you tomorrow after we know more—if there's anymore to find out," Bill promised and then hung up the phone.

"What do you want to do?" Margaret asked after a minute.

Rich didn't answer. He just sat, staring first at his feet, then at her, and then out the window, tears streaming down his face.

"You need to get tested," Margaret whispered.

"How long had she been sick? How long could she have been sick? Maybe I gave it to her. Maybe we've had this for years, and it caught up with her quicker," he said, speaking more to himself than to Margaret.

"You have to get yourself tested," Margaret whispered again—a little louder this time—almost a command.

Rich look at her, tears still running down his face.

"I don't feel anything," he said. "I don't feel sad, I don't feel sorry, and I'm not relieved to hear about her. I just feel sick—empty." He had his head in his hands, bent nearly double in the chair.

Margaret leaned over the desk and picked up the phonebook. She knew she needed to do something before she spoke out loud what she was feeling. She was suddenly angry. Sandy had been dead for almost as long as she had known Rich. She had cost them two years of a relationship. Margaret knew that, just as with her earlier feelings of hatred for Sandy—for what she put Rich through—she had to banish that thought and never let it surface again.

As she flipped through the pages, she seemed to catch his attention.

"Who are you calling?" he asked.

"A guy I—we know," she answered as she dialed the telephone. "Hello, may I speak to Jeremy?" she asked as the call was answered on the second ring.

"Who are you calling?" Rich asked again.

"Hey, Jer. This is Margaret—M from the Firehouse. Listen, Jeremy, I've got a problem. I need to find a place for an HIV test … yes, I've seen the ads in the paper. Are they accurate? How long does it take to get the results? No, is there someplace we could come—a clinic or someplace? Yes—no—it's a long story. Can we come tonight or do we have to wait until tomorrow?" She put her hand over the mouthpiece and turned toward him. "Do you want to go down to the clinic tonight? He'll call them and make the arrangements if you do." Rich nodded his head. "Yes, we'll be there within an hour," she answered. "Okay, thanks—we'll see you there."

"Who was that, and where are we going?"

"You know Jeremy—the tall guy with the crew cut, sort of reddish hair."

Rich shrugged his shoulders.

"He's a counselor at the Gay Men's Health Crisis downtown. He comes in maybe once a week." She started for her bedroom. "We'll take a cab."

"Okay," he said, picking up the phonebook. "I think I should go to Tucson. I wonder if I can get a flight out tonight."

"Why don't you call your parents first? Then the airlines, but don't go tonight. You'll get in too late, and you might as well get a good night's sleep and start off early in the morning. You can still probably be there by breakfast."

Rich shook his head, trying to make a mental list of everything he had to do in the next few hours.

Rich spent a week in Tucson. Sandy's cremains were delivered the day after he arrived, and he helped her parents make the interment arrangements with the cemetery. They had already decided that, unless Rich had other ideas, the urn containing her ashes would be placed in the columbarium in the mausoleum near the place where they had purchased a pair of cemetery lots years before.

As hard as they tried, they could not find any additional information about the circumstances of her death. The lawyer that had initially contacted Bill and Lauren had no more information to give. She had changed her name and social security number. That was why it had been impossible to find her. Rich inquired into the process and was told that she was either a victim of identity theft or domestic violence, and since no one had ever contacted him about the latter, it must have been done on the grounds of a claimed identity theft.

Rich wanted to go to Santa Barbara to meet with the lawyer, but Bill talked him out of it.

"Just let it go," Bill advised. "You tried. God knows you tried. We know that these years have been hell for you—they've been hell for all of us."

"Bill, Lauren, let me tell you something," Rich said, his voice breaking, and tears filling his eyes. "When you called the other night … you told me that I should get tested for HIV and that Margaret should also. Well, we went that night, and I got tested, but Margaret didn't. She didn't need to."

Both of his in-laws looked confused.

"I love Margaret. We have a relationship that's special. Margaret and I have been sharing an apartment, but we've—we haven't been living together—we have never slept together. I know that you thought that we have been—I'm sure that a lot of people—most people think the same. The two of us even laugh and joke about it, but the truth is, until the other night, before you called, I believed that … I believed that I was married to your daughter. Yes, I have fallen in love with another woman, but that's as far as it goes … and I've never …" He couldn't continue.

Bill and Lauren just sat, stunned by the fact that Rich had stayed loyal and faithful all through the years.

"I don't know what to say," Bill finally said, looking at Rich's hand. He was indeed still wearing his wedding ring.

"There's nothing to say. I loved Sandy, and she has been and will always be a part of my life, but again, she hasn't been—she's been gone—she ..." Rich stopped.

"But now that part is over—and, Richard, we hope—we want you to go on with your life. Go back home, and once all of this sinks in, get on with your life—like we thought that you had," Lauren whispered as she hugged him.

A few days later, they drove him to the airport. He promised that he would keep in touch, especially with the results of the test.

He called his parents and then Margaret from the airport while he waited for his plane, telling her when he'd be home and that everything was going to be okay in Arizona—although as much as he had grown to love the place over the years, he was sure that he could never go back. There were too many memories and too many ghosts.

As he hung up the phone, he looked at his hand and the ring, as if he'd never seen it before.

I should have left this here, he thought, and for the first time in so many years, he slipped the ring off of his finger and dropped it into his pocket.

Margaret met him at the airport, and they rode home together on the M-60 bus. Rich had fallen asleep by the time they reached 125th Street and Lexington and transferred to the subway.

Once back in New York, he tried to get back into a normal routine. The people at the firm could not have been better about supporting him. They were happy to have him back and were willing to give him as much time and space as he needed.

It was more difficult at the Firehouse. There were too many familiar faces—people that were sort of like friends but had no idea about what had happened or what was going on. What worried him the most was falling back into the same sort of funk he'd been in for that year and a half after Sandy first left him.

Through it all, he forgot about the results of the blood tests. The letter had arrived a few days after he left for Tucson. Margaret had been to Boston and back, and the envelope had simply been buried in the stack of mail that had accumulated over the week.

Rich found it there when he returned from Tucson, and without opening it, he slipped it into the book he had been reading.

Rich wasn't sure whether he wanted to teach his class at the club on Wednesday night, but Margaret talked him into it. She'd told him that kicking the hell out of a bag would probably do him good. She was right.

The apartment was dark when he came home. Margaret had gone with him but as usual had returned before he did. He was confused by the darkness. It seemed that there wasn't any light coming from the front windows or the skylight. The light in her bedroom wasn't even on.

He thought she had gone to bed. He decided to knock on her door.

"Hey!" she said as he tossed his keys on the table. Rich jumped and had to catch his breath. "Sorry," she whispered.

"What are you doing, sitting in the dark?" Rich asked as he reached for the light switch.

"No, don't—I'm sitting in the dark because you're home early. Come and sit down."

Rich moved around the table, brushing it with his thigh as he made his way toward the sofa. He heard Margaret move her legs and sit up.

"I didn't feel like taking a steam after lifting tonight—I didn't even take a shower, I just came home." He didn't sit on the sofa; he was still wearing his sweat clothes from the gym and was wet. He needed to take a shower and change. He sat on the edge of the coffee table, facing Margaret. Neither of them spoke. He lowered the hood of his sweatshirt.

"You shouldn't have come home in those wet clothes. It's freezing outside. You'll catch your death. You sound tired. You feeling okay?" She reached out and put the back of her hand on his forehead.

Neither of them spoke for a few minutes, but it seemed like an hour.

"Well?" Margaret asked, leaning in and putting her hand on his knee.

"Well what?" Rich answered softly. There had been thousands of questions these past weeks, and he did not know which one Margaret was asking. He had to shake his head to clear it and bring himself back into focus. He didn't intend to sound sardonic, but he knew that was exactly the way it might have sounded.

"What did the test say?" she asked, her voice trembling.

"I don't know. I didn't open it yet."

She moved her hand and stood. "You have to look—you have to know. Where is it?"

"Right there on the table … in the book. I hoped that you'd have looked already."

"I wouldn't have even if I'd known where you'd put it." She bumped the table. "Ouch! Damn!"

"Turn on the light. This is crazy," he said as she rubbed her foot, flipped on the light in the kitchen, and then picked up the envelope from the table.

"You want it over there or over here in the light?"

Rich stood up, feeling like he weighed six hundred pounds, his mouth suddenly going dry, and his knees feeling rubbery. He began to feel sick. He slowly moved toward the kitchen, where Margaret now stood, holding the envelope.

She handed it to him, and he tore it open, taking a deep breath. He read in silence as she bit her lip.

"Negative!" he answered, handing the test results to her as tears began to well up. "I'm going to take a shower."

She watched him walk slowly toward the bathroom, waiting for the door to close before she looked at the letter and then started to cry—the fears of the last ten days coming out in sobs. She gave him a couple of minutes and then followed him into the bathroom. Rich didn't bother completely undressing. He'd taken off only his shoes, sweatpants, sweatshirt, and T-shirt and was standing in his gym shorts and socks with his head under the stream, facing the wall and letting warm water run over his shoulders and down his back. He was standing in the same position he'd been in when she shaved his back—both palms on the wall at shoulder level, with the top of his forehead pressed against the tiles. Margaret stepped out of her slippers and into the shower.

He'd been back for a couple of days, and this was the first time that she noticed he had taken the ring off of his finger.

"Hey," she whispered, putting her arms around his chest, pressing against his back, and laying her head on his shoulder. "Why don't we go out to Montauk Friday afternoon and spend the weekend? It will do you good … it will do me good."

"Yeah, I'd like that … I think," he answered after a minute, taking her hands into his. Her arms tightened around his chest.

"I'd like that too," she whispered as she slipped under his arm and faced him under the shower. "You know, I don't want you to spend just the weekend with me. I'd like you to spend the rest of your life with me. Forever."

"Yeah, I'd like that too—the rest of our lives," he promised, taking her in his arms and crying in spasms with his face buried in her neck. All the years and the past two weeks of unknowing, uncertainty, and anguish came out at once as her embrace brought him back to life … and he was certain that he could feel the bricks move and shift under their feet, drawing them deeper into the Firehouse.